The Speaker
for the Trees

Sean DeLauder

For Laura, Graham, and Symmetry

CONTENTS

We humans look rather different from a tree. Without a doubt we perceive the world differently than an a tree does. But down deep, at the molecular heart of life, the trees and we are essentially identical.

—Carl Sagan

PRELUDE

At the center of a round table was a bonsai plant in a shallow but wide pot—a miniature tree twisted into place and deformed like an over-tightened screw. Two people sat on opposite sides of the table, each watching the other while the plant watched them both in mute fascination, listening. The plant was only dimly aware of the world around it, its thoughts tiny and fleeting, centered mostly around a childlike want for light or water, but the bonsai knew the woman was named Anna and the man was named Hedge.

The bonsai was not smart when compared to most plants, content just to *be* rather than to *be something*, but it seemed clear to the bonsai that Hedge had as much in common with the bonsai as he did with the woman, and that struck the bonsai as peculiar. This peculiarity was a source of endless curiosity for the bonsai, for it made the plant wonder what Hedge was doing here, how he could seem to be one thing and yet be another, and what the purpose of his strangeness might be.

There were things a bonsai could never hope to fathom, like simple arithmetic or crossword puzzles, but it took great pleasure in knowing it was in the presence of something remarkable, some unspoken profundity that no one else could detect, but the bonsai could feel. It was the electric tension of anticipation, those heightened moments in a normal person's day before they are interrupted by the unexpected shock of an amazing discovery that leaves them changed forever.

So the bonsai listened, and watched, sensing the gathering storm and waiting for the bolt to strike.

SIGN

Hedge was fat.

His round, sagging body stretched a short-sleeved shirt with faint yellow stains in the armpits, and his skin, which had a faintly greenish tint, was dark and peeled on the back of his neck and the top of his head from spending long hours under the sun. Fat and bald, but not slobbery and sloppy. Hedge could be best described, in most respects, as ordinary.

The perfect disguise.

No one suspected he was a plant sent to the planet by the legendary Plant of Ultimate Knowing to observe humanity and, if necessary, protect them from one of countless interstellar perils, such as bursts of interstellar radiation, drifting planetoids, invading space armies, or appearances by the infamous Visitors. No one he told took him seriously. Of all the armors built around protecting his identity, the most formidable by far was incredulity.

Of the many perils, the peril of Visitors was utmost. Visitors were a mysterious species who wandered the cosmos, spreading destruction wherever they set foot. They had been here before, in fact, hundreds of millions of years ago. Soon after, the planet suffered a catastrophic rhinoplasty at the hands of a comet that altered the planetary ecosystem, shifting the balance of dominance from reptiles to mammals. But these appearances were rare. As best as Hedge could tell, the greatest threat to humanity was a persistent volatile nature it had yet to outgrow.

For the moment, Hedge's only mission was to remain hidden. A mission could change at any moment, but this one had remained the same for 20 years.

Hedge regarded the plate before him with resignation. It was empty with exception to a small, triangular pork chop, but it seemed a larger task for one who had labored on several offerings already. He took a breath, straining the buttons on his shirtfront, then let it out in a long, quiet sigh.

Across the small kitchen table sat Hedge's round, unthreatening earth wife, Anna. It pleased him to know she was highly symmetrical. After all, it was in symmetry that humans found beauty, and to know that she was beautiful gave him a very human sense of pride and accomplishment in having something other humans desired.

She stared back at him with a furrowed brow and pressed lips. Her eyes flicked from his face to his unmoving hands clenched around the flatware, to the plate, and back again. He knew she was worrying that his ulcers were boiling or that he didn't enjoy the pork chops. These worries were, of course, completely ridiculous.

Ulcers were an impossibility since Hedge processed light into energy and had no stomach. Whether he liked the pork chops or not was irrelevant because he had no taste buds and stored food in an empty vacuole for later disposal. So he stared back at her, absorbing the expression and tracing her face with his eyes. People appreciated that. Paying attention. They also appreciated the opportunity to express their concerns, so Hedge indulged her in typical human fashion.

"What?" he asked in a nasal tone tinged with annoyance.

He forked a bit of pork chop, pulled it off with his teeth and felt it tumble down his neck tube and drop into the heap of bits in his bulging middle part.

"Something is the matter," she said, her forehead creased. "You seem... I don't know. Strange."

For all their simplicity, humans could be remarkably perceptive, though they didn't know it most of the time, and their ability to thrust straight through deception and see to the heart of truth was often lost with childhood. By adulthood humans had trained themselves to be coy and manipulative in response to the coy and manipulative society in which they lived, which led them to believe that everyone was trying to be as coy and manipulative as themselves and were uncertain about what was true and what was not. Beyond their few flashes of clarity, everything became a muddle of colliding doubts.

Hedge wiped a wadded napkin across his chin.

"Well," he began.

He'd explained this before. Each time the same response. A roll of her eyes, a grimace, and a shrug. Why did he bother indulging her? It may have been love, but from his studies he knew other humans felt a strong upwelling of sensation when they loved. A swelling of chemicals such as oxytosine and vasopressin in the brain and blood that Hedge did not experience because he had xylem and phloem tissues that moved fluids through a decentralized and essentially brainless body. There was no primary nerve cluster where all thoughts gathered. There were no hormones that gushed from a pituitary gland to elate him, make his heart beat faster, and rush them through his circulatory system to touch the outermost reaches of his inner spaces. Only nutrients ferrying through his body to prevent the tissue from becoming dry, dark, and dead.

"I'm not really from this planet, but I'm here to protect it. For the plants. No one expects trouble, but if there were something cataclysmic, a transdimensional war whose proximity jeopardized this planet for example, you should be safe with me, earth wife." He paused, allowing her to consider, and took another bite. "You know," he added around a mouthful of pork chop, "I don't even have a stomach."

She blinked, mouth falling crookedly ajar. Then, as expected, her eyes screwed in a quick circle. She stood, pushed in the chair, and lifted her plate.

"You think everything is a joke," she said.

She didn't suspect anything. No one did. With exception to Scud Peabody, but he was a genius.

As far as Anna was concerned they had met at a squaredance in Topeka. They talked long into the night. She invited him to dinner and he enjoyed her pork chops. Two months later they were married. Hedge took a loan, bought a house on a wide plot. He tended beehives and they didn't sting him. She made pork chops. He ate them. It was love. That was their story.

A history that had been penciled onto the tablet of her memory during her abduction. They did this every so often, rewrote a bit of someone's past, usually when they wanted to insert an operative into the social fabric of a community. A human cohort, they had found, lent much to the deception.

At the moment her back was to him, ponderous backside swaying arhythmically as she bent over the sink and scrubbed at the stubborn stains of a coffee mug. She was better this way. Hidden from a violent past, abusive parents. She'd been unhappy, wandering through a forest in the rain when they found her, bruised and bleeding inside, afraid to go back home. It was easier to scribble over memories a person didn't want to remember, so they searched for these people—the abused and neglected. They repaired her insides, repaired her sundered mind. Now those memories were gone.

Hedge looked to his plate, the wide slab of meat staring back at him in all its enormity, and felt the uncomfortable weight of too many chunks already inside him. Once, in a similar predicament, he had regurgitated the pork chops onto the table in a warm stew of ragged chunks, but that had made Anna cry. He had yet to find an equally effective manner of emptying himself since, but the sight of Anna in tears flooded him with a sense of wrongness.

There was a bonsai plant in the center of the table, a solemn and tiny tree that always seemed to be watching him. Even now he felt it was staring at him, waiting for him to make a decision. So he lifted the plate, stretched his face around the porcelain while she wasn't looking, and dumped everything into his gullet. The stretching heaviness in his middle became unbearable. He needed to purge.

The chair scrubbed across the floor when he stood.

"I'm walking," he said, then added an appreciative belch in afterthought. "Uuurp."

Earth wife Anna fluttered her fingers above a shoulder and Hedge passed through the living room and out the front door of their two-story farmhouse. The house stood inside a white rail fence Hedge had constructed, beside a wooden barn whose weathered boards were turning gray, and a corn field beyond.

She would find the empty plate and be happy. Then she would curl in bed beside him, read a few pages of a dull story and fall asleep. She would do the same if she were angry, but she would not enjoy the story, would not drop off to sleep. Her mind would flutter and despair and wake up harried. It took him a great long while to realize the reason for this was that she loved him. It took still longer to realize she wanted him to love her in return. And one of the larger parts of love involved consuming pork chops.

His midsection burbled angrily.

Love was invariably harder some times than others.

The screen door whined and smacked shut behind him as Hedge lumbered across the porch and down the steps, walked beside the bed of dipped, snoozing flowers that traced the house and crunched across the gravel drive on the way to the barn.

It was a cool night, with gentle breezes that knocked solitary, ringing notes from the porch wind chime. A full moon stared down at everything with an expression of permanent awe, bright enough that Hedge could see the swooping black boomerangs of bats as they swung back and forth over the small pond behind the house. Bees droned dully in their hives, fat and sated by a hard day's work.

Hedge unfastened his pants and let them slide to his ankles, knees bent with his back against the shrub-ringed barn, feeling the weight inside him shift as he prepared to empty his vacuole behind a bush in an act many humans referred to as "taking a dump" where the raccoons would find it. It was a confusing tangle of words since he wasn't taking, but giving. There was scarcely enough room to take any more. Then a flash of light silhouetted him, pants down, against the side of the barn. Long enough to draw his attention from the current process.

It came from the cornfield.

"Hedgelford Bran Johnston!" cried the earth wife from the kitchen window. Her tone was raking and furious, a tone used in conjunction with his full name only when deadly serious—a frightful state that sometimes rattled even Hedge, which was strange because humans were largely undangerous when compared to the evolutionary paths other creatures had taken. Notably, the Fire-tailed Xiz, which could detach and launch exploding parts of its body at prey, attackers, and its own insubordinate children. "Get your pants up, this *instant!*"

Earthfolk were fundamentally modest, clothing the majority of their flesh under the pretense of preventing chills. And rightly so. The majority were hideously misshapen, flesh drooping from their bodies like broad, baggy coat pockets turned inside out. His own shape had a peculiar tentacle in the midsection for which he had yet to find a use except to drain a reservoir of waste fluid, though his earth wife found it fascinating. Oddly enough, oftentimes so did Hedge, and he didn't mind indulging her.

This time he was too distracted to obey.

Ignoring her calls, Hedge stared into the field. Sure enough, the light came again—a bright white pillar of cold brilliance that struck in the center of the field, throwing thin shadows against the ground. Hedge took a step forward. And fell in the dirt, legs caught in the pants he hadn't bothered to draw up. Fitting irony.

Jerking the pants to his waist, Hedge ran to the house, flashed past a scowling Anna and up the stairs as quickly as the torpid body would allow. He banged open the bathroom door and pulled the drapes aside to stare into the cornfield. And there they were, visible in the moonlight. Patterns flattened into the crops as though a giant had stretched a foot out of the heavens to stomp frantically after an invasion of scrambling cockroaches. To anyone else they were an unintelligible jumble of circles and tangled lines like the brambles of an impassable briar patch. To Hedge they were words, instructions, a message he understood in an eyeblink.

Danger. Immediate recall and report.

Danger from what, he wondered. Supernova? Solar radiation? Visitors? Hedge exhaled a deep, shuddering breath.

He was going to need a toaster.

MR. VISITOR

"You know they're here, don't you?"

Burt blinked, clearing the blur from his eyes as he emerged from a gentle half sleep brought on by staring into the campfire and feeling its warmth lick his face. He looked down and saw he was seated on the overturned bucket he'd used to carry fish from the boat. Blearily, he looked to his left and saw the shimmer of stars on the lake. He watched the descending moon and its reflection creep toward one another, wondering if they would bounce when they met and go caroming off in some unexpected direction, then felt a poke in his ribs.

He turned back to the right and found Clem, hat crushed down to his eyes, a few inches from his face. He appeared to be waiting for something.

"Who's here?" Burt responded at last.

Clem sat back. Pointed to the ground.

"People what watch us at night when we're sleepin'. People what ain't really people, but they look like us and talk like us and smell like us. Studyin' us. They don't like what we done with this place."

"Who?"

Burt looked around the campsite. He studied the low-hanging trees, but didn't see anything out of place.

Clem leaned in close and answered the question with a gust of fish-smelling breath.

"Mole folk."

Burt's eyes hooked back to Clem.

"Mole folk?" Burt repeated.

Clem had subjected Burt to his bizarre conspiracy theories before. Clem had once claimed the trees were telling his wife, Thistle, he'd been at the Bus Stop Bar instead of helping Burt patch a pontoon on their boat. He stuck to this theory even after the bartender of the Bus Stop Bar called his wife to come and collect him after he'd passed out in the entrance.

"Was the damned trees," Clem told him a few days later. "They's pivved at me 'cause I nicked their roots with the mower the other day. I done ought to cut 'em down, but then the wife would know I's onto her. They're in cahoots, you know."

Everything that seemed normal to anyone else seemed suspicious to Clem. Lately, anything out of the ordinary was the work of an insidious group of tiny-eyed, subterranean ground diggers that somehow had the ability to look just like people and were always causing mischief that might otherwise have happened of its own accord.

"There ain't no damned mole folk, Clem," said Burt. "Ain't nobody watchin' us. Ain't nobody that look like us, talk like us, or smell like us that ain't us. The only folk out here is you and me."

Burt jabbed a finger at Clem, then himself for emphasis.

In response, Clem raised a hand and pointed past Burt.

"And that feller."

Burt turned. Sure enough, a man stood behind him, looking from one of them to the other, an enormous smile on his face.

He was dressed in a black suit and tie, carried no camping gear, and wore sunglasses beneath a tree-shaded night sky. His skin was as chalky white as the moon behind him. The smile on his face was unwavering, unnaturally large, and didn't sit quite straight, like the fissure in a broken watermelon. It might have been any of these oddities that drew their attention, but it was the stainless steel toaster he held in both hands that caught their gazes, and they watched in awe as their distended reflections grew and shrank on its silvery surface.

Burt and Clem exchanged glances with the visitor, then with each other. Finally, Clem broke the silence.

"What is that?" he asked.

The visitor followed Clem's gaze to his hands.

"This," said the visitor, with a voice deep with gravity, "is a toaster."

"Oh," said Clem, disappointed.

"Not what he expected," Burt explained.

"What did he expect?"

"Just that," said Clem. "But... not that."

"Something more," explained Burt.

The visitor appeared perplexed.

"I see," said the visitor, not seeing.

"I'm Burt," said Burt. "This one's Clem. Can we help you?"

"Yes," said the visitor. "Yes you can. My name is..." The visitor paused in thought for a moment. "Mr. Visitor. I'm looking for someone. Maybe more than someone. Do you know anyone around here who behaves... strangely?"

Burt jerked a thumb back toward Clem.

"Certifiable," he said.

Clem smacked Burt's hand away.

"This might be serious, jackass."

"There's another fellow in Greenville always saying weird stuff," added Burt. "Like how he's a plant or somethin'."

Mr. Visitor tensed.

"A plant?" he asked.

"Yeah," said Burt. "Hedge Johnston. Farmer. Bee keeper. Pretty ordinary guy. Other than the crazy stuff, I guess."

"Always talkin' to that moonbat, Scud," Clem added.

"What manner of creature is a moonbat?" asked Mr. Visitor.

"Vegetable, maybe," said Burt, considering.

"I see," said Mr. Visitor. "Greenville. This is the name of the civilian center where Hedge dwells, correct? Can you tell me where I can find it?"

"That way," said Burt, pointing. "Ten miles."

"Twelve," Clem corrected.

Burt turned around, annoyed.

"The hell difference do two miles make?"

"Reckon it makes a two-mile difference, don't it?"

Burt huffed and turned again to face Mr. Visitor, but as abruptly as he'd arrived, he was gone again. A faint scent of burnt toast hung on the air for an instant before a sudden gust took it away.

"I betcha he'ns one of 'em," said Clem quietly.

"One a who?"

"Mole people."

Burt scowled and hunched toward the fire.

"Shut up, Clem."

BACKGROUND FIRST, THEN A TOASTER

Scud Peabody was a genius. Of that Hedge was certain.

He'd come to the conclusion earlier in the day while seated beside Scud at Milo's Corner Diner, before it became obvious he was going to need a toaster.

Milo's Corner Diner was an unimaginative self description with broad windows on two sides that faced the streets. A perpetual greasy haze hung about the ceiling and the place smelled of hot sausage and syrup. The walls were a sickly, off yellow like the watered-down orange juice and a ceiling fan with a broken blade jerked lazily all year round.

"You don't l... look like a plant," Scud stuttered. He did this sometimes, and his whole face squinted in an effort to get a word past his lips.

Scud Peabody was a scruffy, skinny, troll of a man whose eyes bulged from his head like mushroom bulbs at the end of their stalks, jerking from one object to the next, his mind a constantly spinning carousel of jangling, obnoxious thought. He had a baggy, hound-dog face with a stubbly mouth always hanging open.

"Exactly," said Hedge. "I'm in disguise."

Scud Peabody was the only person who believed Hedge was a plant alien because Scud Peabody was the only person wide minded enough to do so. Because he was so wide minded it only made sense that everyone thought Scud was an idiot.

"Scud, yer an idjit," sneered Garry Thorne from a table by the window. "He's jerkin' yer chain."

Garry Thorne was an unemployed truck driver who spent most of his time at the diner, sneering at Scud or anyone else who caught his attention. He sneered at the waitress who took his order, sneered at the fellows who sat at the table with him, sneered at his children who would inherit his sneer and be

9

hated by everyone around them. And people did hate Garry Thorne. But they also knew that to not be an ally of Garry Thorne was to be his victim. Most people tacitly agreed to permit cruelty rather than risk being subject to it.

Which was why Scud Peabody, who did not join them, who cultivated his own opinions and did not fear the regular chastisement of Garry Thorne, was a genius. And because Scud was a genius Hedge knew there was no point trying to deceive him.

"Ye ain't l... lyin' to m... m... me, is ya?"

Scud's distended eyeballs bulged imploringly.

"Plants don't lie," said Hedge.

Scud considered this.

"Ain't posin' as a p... person a lie?" he asked.

Hedge wondered how no one else could tell that Scud was a genius.

"It *is* deception," Hedge explained. "But for the purpose of self preservation. Some birds pantomime a broken wing to lure predators away from their young. Some moths disguise themselves with the pattern of poisonous insects. Some insects take on the appearance of sticks in an effort to blend into their surroundings. But they, like myself, behave so in order to survive. Should we come out of obscurity there is no shortage of scientists who would be interested in studying *us* instead of the other way round, which would be a great hindrance to the mission."

"Ain't tellin' *me* about it d... dangerous?"

"Idjit!" came another cry, not Garry Thorne this time, followed by a few broken cackles.

"No one believes me," said Hedge. "It's doubtful anyone would believe you."

Scud smiled.

"You s... sure is smart, Hedge. I wonders why you ain't a fancy s... scientist off in a labbertory inventin' gadgets to make life easy fer rich folk. Think that's what I would d... d... do if I were so smart as you and not so s... soft in the p... pate."

Hedge liked Scud a great deal. He was blunt and unassuming, and his character was louder than his mouth. He took an interest in those who required aid, from steadying the waitress who struggled to carry her order, to bringing grubs to the hatchlings nesting in the crook of the main window.

"You fecktard," crowed Garry Thorne. "Course he's lying. Birds ain't smart. They brains ain't no more powerful 'n yours. An' you're about as smart as a sock full o' nickels."

A chorus of laughter ensued. Scud's eyes never left Hedge while they laughed, as though so long as he held a gaze with someone else he was invincible because they didn't exist. Hedge returned the gaze until the laughter and jibes ebbed and Scud asked another question.

It was a long time.

In addition to being stupid, Scud was also a boy-teasing faggot, albino shithead, mutant retard and as many other combinations as Garry and the others could imagine because, as it seemed to Hedge, they were all so terribly jealous of his brilliance, and infuriated by his curiosity and the idea that he didn't give one whit about their opinion.

That was how Hedge knew Scud was not an idiot. Most distinguishable about the idiot, Hedge noted, was their fear of that which was different. Those who feared difference always made a point of finding difference in others in order to feel more secure in their sameness. They referred to other people as fags, retards, et cetera. They also had names for those of different social class, those who dwelled in different regions of their country and the world, names for people depending on their job, depending on their hair color, skin color, religion, intelligence, and any other characteristic that made a person distinct. It seemed to Hedge that by process of elimination the only people they didn't categorically despise was themselves. Of course, there was a name for this as well.

"So why are y... you here?" Scud had asked. "What's your m... m... mission?"

Hedge relished the opportunity to tell someone besides Anna, but knew he couldn't possibly explain everything and be home in time to eat pork chops. So Hedge summarized.

* * *

Hedge was born (as it were) in a government nursery on the bright side of the unspinning greenhouse planet Krog-B alongside ten thousand of his kin, all neatly arranged in hundreds of parallel rows like strips of soybeans. The metaphor was appropriate, since Hedge was himself a plant, albeit far more complex than a soybean. Hedge was the acme of a species that had existed longer than the simplest forms of life on the human planet, developing over time into a hardy species of considerable cognitive might and universal significance.

Humanity had undergone a similar transformation over the course of their existence, but with less impressive results. Being that each human born could be considered the result of thousands upon thousands of years of evolution and natural selection, there must be a universal sense of disappointment due to their striking lack of achievement.

Plants had discovered this planet long before the existence of humanity. Because mammals had never played more than a minor role on other planets no one suspected they would ever be more than a few warm-blooded rats and badgers scurrying through the scrub and living underground. When plants first visited, dinosaurs appeared to be the dominant species, though it was clear it would only be a matter of time before plants evolved and became their masters. There was no corner of the globe to which plants had not spread. Algae and photosynthetic protozoa in the oceans stood to be the first steps in mobile plantlife; long grasses spread across the plains and trees bunched themselves into continent-wide forests; even deserts had been infiltrated by cacti and scruffy shrubbery, showing the plantlife of this planet was highly adaptable and would not be impeded in their march toward complete domination. Plants were so prolific there were even plants growing on plants—mosses and fungi and crawling vines that wrapped themselves around trunks like badly knotted laces.

At the time of this survey the explorers raised the question of whether life forms on this planet should be eliminated in case they developed greater sentience, but these notions were disregarded. Certainly dinosaurs were not intelligent enough to rule the planet, but they were too dumb to do it much damage either.

Thus the explorers departed, scheduling a return after a sufficient number of eons passed. This would allow the plants time to develop into a species better able to communicate with their off-world brethren and join the Federation of Floral Planets.

Imagine the shock of these explorers when they returned, hundreds of millions of years later, to find the docile dinosaurs gone and a heretofore unheard of primate race thriving. Plants remained utterly immobile, largely insentient, and for the most part indifferent about their low status on the planet. They were pets in many cases, kept indoors which stunted their growth and kept them hidden from nurturing sunlight. In other cases they were grown in abundance, only to be harvested by the millions to satisfy the primates' ballooning population.

There was a cry of outrage amongst the council members urging mobilization of an army to destroy humanity and restore the planet to plants. The outrage increased after evidence surfaced that the Visitors had arrived on the planet not long before the dinosaurs had been destroyed. Plants knew little of the Visitors other than they were a dwindling spacefaring civilization whose appearance always meant trouble.

After a long debate between the council and the Plant of Ultimate Knowing, it was decided destroying humanity would be hasty, impatient, and impolite. More to the point, the Plant argued, it would be unwise to hand control of a planet to plants which had not seized it for themselves in the first place. Instead, on the advice of the Plant of Ultimate Knowing, humanity was put under constant surveillance to determine whether or not this slowly blooming species was truly dangerous. Perhaps their emergence was a fortunate fluke. Maybe humanity could show plants something they had overlooked in their many millennia of dominance.

So it had been many more hundreds of years. Gradually, as human technology improved, plants had to alter their strategies. At first plants settled into the community as stationary trees, observing from forests. Others were potted plants, watching through the windows. Then, as their understanding of humanity improved, plants were able to infiltrate human society itself, as Hedge had done, appearing no different from humans on the outside, though their physiology remained largely plantlike.

At this point in the explanation Scud interrupted, asking Hedge a question with little pertinence, but filled with meaning. Which was just the sort of unexpectedness he had come to expect from Scud Peabody. Genius, in all its fascinating manifestations, never ceased to take others by surprise.

"So. D... do you l... like it here?"

The question puzzled Hedge for a moment. Why wouldn't Scud want to hear about the physiological differences between humans and plants? It was a fascinating subject, especially when one considered the numerous modifications invented so plants and humans could interact on an intimate level. Hedge's peculiar tentacle came to mind.

Scud's expression was imploring, just as Anna tended to be when she watched him eat pork chops. Then Hedge understood. More than anything, more than they cared about knowledge, humanity wanted to be liked. Those who had a deeper understanding of their purpose, of their existence, wanted to know if they were doing well because they really weren't sure of themselves. Unlike Garry Thorne, whose stubbornness would doom him to a lifetime of making others miserable and causing them to dislike him, some people were willing to change if they felt they were going astray.

So Hedge pondered. And, to Hedge's amazement, found that he did like this place. He hadn't much thought about it before. He enjoyed his piddling chores and the feathery warmth of the yellow star touching him between the places where bees crawled across his body. Liked dealing with the silly trivialities of existence: folding towels, oiling squeaky hinges, repainting the rusty weathervane. Liked all these things because they were tedious, and he knew it could all be much, much worse.

Existence on the human planet was quite different from existence with other plants. Humanity was social and intimate. Where he originated there was no wife who doted upon him nor cared about his happiness. Only a female with megagametophytes a thousand miles away to which his pollen drifted. If nothing else, Hedge admired the human fondness for meaningful, close relationships. It created passionate stirrings in them, which unfortunately also led to confrontation, arguments, and conflict—a double-edged sword which manifested in his relationship with Anna.

She grew stern when other femme humans turned their attention on him, and sterner still when he returned it. When Penny Grobshire asked how his rose bushes grew so thick with blossoms in the ShopMart Anna glared from the end of the aisle while he explained. Fertilizer and sun and water are all well and good, but they mean little when the flowers know you aren't

13

genuinely concerned about their welfare. One cannot just want them to be beautiful, one has to know they are already beautiful and they need only show it. Why no one understood plants had emotions and nursed feelings of neglect Hedge could not understand.

Anna stiffened when Penny touched his shoulder in thanks, an oddly affecting human means of appreciation, and was quiet the rest of the day.

Eventually Hedge realized it made Anna sad not to have him to herself. This was not immediately clear, but took a great deal of probing and extrapolation since humanity had the bewildering tendency to be conspicuous when they were emoting, weeping, huffing, or scowling, but subtle and evasive about why. He found it touching that one human could care so much about another that they were physically and emotionally distraught by the possibility of losing that person's affection. At the same time Hedge found increasingly that he enjoyed pleasing Anna. He wondered, even without the upwelling of strong emotions, if this constituted something like love.

So Hedge began growing more of himself around the waist—something most folk found unattractive. At the physical age of thirty-five he stopped growing hair but for a semi-circle around his head. Women stopped asking about the flowers and Anna was happy.

Yes, he answered. Yes, he did like it here and would be sad should he have to leave.

Scud seemed very pleased by this admission and beamed mightily, his eyes glassy, faltering for only a moment when Garry Thorne poured salt on his flapjacks. It didn't matter. Because as a genius, Scud knew humanity was doing well in the eyes of the Universe, and that was far more important than a stack of salty flapjacks.

And such was Hedge's existence. Watching people. Waiting for instructions. Eating pork chops.

Until recently. Now he had orders to report as soon as possible.

It was for this reason Hedge needed a toaster.

A VERY HANDY DEVICE

The scattered guts of a disassembled toaster lay before Hedge on the kitchen table. Springs and heating coils, levers and clamps and clasps, bread holsters and the reflective chrome shell. Now that he had it apart he could begin putting it back together—with a few crucial changes.

Curious how one arrangement of such simple components yielded a starkly different device. It was as though the toaster were an anagram for something else, just as the word Horse could be rearranged into Shore, though, he noted, one could not make a Shore by rearranging the parts of a Horse. Were people to see what Hedge was doing, the few places where parts were exchanged, they would undoubtedly shake their heads, flabbergasted by their inability to see the obvious: that such a trivial device could unlock the cosmos.

They would be full of bluster and arrogance and mutter things like *Well it's quite clear to me...* and *It was right there all the time* and...

"Oh my."

Well, probably not so much that phrase, but something similarly meaningless.

"Oh my," Anna repeated from the living room.

It was the noon hour when the local news aired on the television. Anna never failed to inform herself of the latest calamities. Humanity, for all its high ideals, for all its despair at the notion of suffering, was addicted to disaster. There was nothing more delightful, more utterly soul stirring than to learn of another person's tragic miseries. The more miserable, the more cathartic. If other people were miserable, their own existence was by comparison much better. Theirs was a perpetual quest for someone to pity, be it children orphaned by floodwaters, victims of a helicopter crash, soldiers and insurgents clashing in some faraway country, or, as was most often the case, themselves.

"Hedgelford?"

Hedge huffed. Interruptions, by their nature, always came when he was in the middle of something important.

"Yes?" Hedge responded gruffly.

"Didn't you buy a toaster this morning?"

Hedge cast a grim look across the strewn pieces of metal and plastic before him.

"Yes," he said still more gruffly, knowing there was another question to come, hoping his tone would stop her pestering.

It didn't.

"Were there a lot of people getting toasters?"

"Because I need it in order to report back to the Council of..." He stopped. "What?"

It wasn't the question he expected. He'd anticipated Why? Why buy a toaster? That seemed the obvious question.

Now Hedge could hear the high-pitched, urgent prattling typical of the news program, designed to create anxiety and suggest that no matter where one was, no matter how secure, they were always within reach of disaster.

... recent run on the most pedestrian of appliances: the Toaster.

Hedge shoved himself away from the table and lumbered into the living room where Anna sat on the sofa, bent forward and tight-mouthed, concentrating. Hedge stood beside the coffee table in front of the couch, arms crossed, and stared intently at the television.

On screen was a sunny reporter in a yellow rain slicker with a microphone in one hand and an umbrella in the other. Hedge expected to see car wreckage or a burning building in the background. Instead he saw the familiar parking lot and façade of the supermarket, untouched by tragedy or destruction. Another shape wavered off camera, occasionally appearing in larger chunks as it shifted anxiously from one foot to the other.

We visited a local Greenville ShopMart to ask: Why the sudden need for toast? With us on this gloomy day is bright-eyed shopper, John Elm. So, John. Why the need for toasters?

The view turned from the reporter to a tall, thick-chested man with wild brown hair and fat caterpillars for eyebrows. He was somewhat stooped and gnarled within the confines of muscle and a plaid flannel shirt. Looking tiny in his hands was a box with a dramatized photo of a toaster blasting toasted bread from its slots which exploded into fireworks to the delight of two excited children.

Hedge's eyes widened. John Elm was almost certainly a plant agent. How many had been sent the message? How many had been summoned back?

John blinked, gazing blankly into the camera, then realized it was his cue to speak.

It's a very handy device, he explained, forcing an uncertain smile. The camera continued to hang on him for an uncomfortable moment before realizing he wasn't going to continue. John, thinking his obligation fulfilled, made as if to be on his way, but the reporter corralled him with her umbrella.

How so? the reported persisted.

Simple, John answered, perhaps thinking if he were to answer quickly he could escape. *They make possible the very complex process of...* John stopped abruptly in mid sentence, knowing he was on the verge of making a colossal admission but not knowing how to back out of it. His eyes were large and unfocused, darting here and there for something that might save him. *Uh*, he stammered, looking uneasy. Again he tried to step from beneath the umbrella to the comfort of rain but found himself blocked. Hedge tensed. He was going to say it, to admit to all humanity how close they were to instantaneous interstellar transportation. All the universe would be open to people. For good or evil, Hedge wasn't sure.

Toasting bread? the reporter suggested.

John's eyes fell to the toaster, then returned sheepishly to the camera.

Yes.

Hedge released a long breath of air, not realizing he'd been holding it.

Without another word, John Elm hurried away. The reporter appeared confused by his sudden departure and looked as though she would make a grab at him before collecting herself and turning back to the camera, bright teeth exposed.

There you have it, folks. From east to west, north to south, America loves toast!

The view returned to the newsroom where two anchors laughed at the observation with practiced mirth.

Nation wide! This was more serious than Hedge thought.

"Isn't that strange?" asked Anna. "Like there was some sort of subliminal message that made everyone run off to get toasters. It makes me uncomfortable. Like there is something dreadful going on in plain sight, but I can only see the shadows."

She tapped her fingernails against her teeth. Hedge knew this meant she was nervous. At the same time he knew how to calm her.

"Do not be fearful, earth wife," said Hedge. Anna looked up at him, waiting for him to continue. "No harm will come to you."

She gave him a half smile.

"You're always so weirdly sincere," she said. "I guess I love you for that."

The half smile found its other half and became full, but she was staring at him in the intense, patient way that told him she was waiting for something. Not just something, an equal acknowledgement of the love which she had just expressed.

Hedge thought a moment, then smiled in return.

"I find you highly symmetrical."

* * *

It was late in the evening already and it would be later still before Hedge would complete reconfiguring the toaster. Anna sat in the seat across from him, head cradled in her hands, watching as he screwed a part in here, broke a piece off there and tossed it aside. She tried to help as best she could, handing over instruments as he called for them like a nurse passing clamps and scalpels to a surgeon, without the least idea of what he was doing.

"I could toast bread on the stove for you," said Anna. "Why do you need a toaster?"

"I don't want toast," said Hedge.

Anna considered this, but didn't ask the obvious question. Not that she would have believed the answer. She picked up two pieces of the toaster, a small spring and a dark plastic part and attempted to join them. After passing several minutes without success she set them down and looked across the table as though scanning for parts that looked like they would fit with one another.

"Why don't you just take it back to the store?" she asked.

Hedge didn't look up. Almost finished.

"I can fix it," he answered.

"For what? It's past bed time. We need to be up early. Tomorrow is morning service. Look at the mess you've made."

It was true. The table, and much of the floor around the table, was covered with scraps Hedge deemed useless and pushed away. Bits of black plastic, cardboard packaging, instructions, warranty details, the crumb tray. Even his hands were slick with the grease from the moving parts.

"It doesn't matter," Hedge replied.

Anna stiffened. Her face bent into a scowl. Hedge couldn't see it, since he was concentrating on the toaster, but after a moment of silence he could feel the animosity. When he looked up she was standing, face red, fists balled at her sides.

Hedge blinked.

Were he a mammal his heart would surely be pounding in his chest, various glands shooting adrenaline to his muscles should he need to flee or defend himself. But he was a plant, and a plant's response to danger was to stay in one spot, remain perfectly still, and hope to be overlooked. So Hedge stayed put.

"You are *not* going to leave this mess for me!" growled his trembling earth wife. "Not after I cleaned this house and yard all day long while you've dickered around with that... that..." She floundered, searching for a terrible curse, but couldn't think of one. "Toaster! It's not right! It's not fair! Oh!" She stomped a foot, unable to express her rage in words. Her eyes darted about as though searching for something to tear in half, but knew it would just contribute to the mess. "Oh! You've gotten me so upset! I don't like being upset! It makes me think awful, frightening things."

Hedge hefted himself from the chair and stood before Anna, whose beet red face was full of distress. He put a hand on her cheek and she leaned into it, believing it was an expression of affection, and her heavy breathing began to slow from the angry puffs that gusted from her nostrils. This was a potentially dangerous situation for her, as undue stress could burst the stitching that held back her old memories just as surely as sutures on a fresh wound could pop free and allow blood to seep through. If that happened, the entire illusion would fall apart, which wouldn't be so much a danger to Hedge since no one would believe her memory had been created by plant aliens. But Anna would be shattered psychologically and shunned socially because she would know a truth no one could ever believe and no one could ever make her deny because denying truth meant one could not believe in anything. And belief and hope were, aside from water, oxygen molecules, and key nutrients, what kept people alive. Her life would be a ruin, and Hedge could not find it in himself to be so cruel to a creature to which he had become so… attached.

Long ago, when they had rewritten her past, they had also inserted a safety valve to allow Hedge to depart if needed without alarming her. It was like a reset button on a stopwatch that returned everything to zero so it could start over again. They did the same for all agents to prevent the sort of pandemonium and suspicion that might result if he just went missing. Placing a hand on her face was just the triggering process. He'd never expected to use it. Now he just needed to speak the words.

"I'm going to visit my brother Edwin in New Jersey," he said. "I'll be back in a week."

Her eyes lazed and her face slackened in his hand.

"… back in a week," she repeated airily.

"Yes," said Hedge. "Why don't you go to bed. You look tired. I'll clean this mess."

"Tired," agreed Anna, turning away. She entered the living room where the stairs led to the second floor and their bedroom. Then stopped. Turned back, her expression perplexed. "You don't have a brother Edwin."

Hedge met her gaze, which bored into him with perfect clarity. He scratched his head.

"Yes I do."

"No," said Anna, walking back toward him. "You don't." She stepped on a scrap of metal and her eyes fell to the kitchen floor. "Oh! Look at the mess!"

As she passed him to survey the debris, Hedge reached out a hand and touched her face.

"I'm going to visit my brother Edwin in New Jersey," he repeated, a bit more sternly. "I'll be back in a week."

Again her eyes clouded and her body slouched.

"Back in a week," she agreed.

She left the kitchen groggily and approached the stairs.

Hedge sat down again, picked up a screwdriver and was about to pry open a small gear box to expose the wiring when she came back.

"Oh!" she exclaimed. "Would you look at this kitchen!"

Hedge stood, turned, and reached a hand out to her face, but she caught it.

"Look at your hands. They're filthy. And don't you wipe them on the dishtowels. This is horrible! I worked for hours to tidy up that linoleum, and now look at it. All covered in bits of metal and plastic."

"I'll get it!" Hedge snapped, jabbed a hand back toward the stairs. "Go to sleep!"

"No need to be snippy," said Anna. She gave him a long look, then went upstairs. "Maybe it's you who needs to get some sleep."

No, thought Hedge. No sleep tonight. Tonight he would be going home.

* * *

Hedge stood at the foot of the bed, the toaster cradled under one arm. It didn't look any different, still silver and toaster-shaped, though it was certainly changed. He wasn't wearing shoes since he wouldn't need them. He didn't really require clothing either, but for some reason he didn't feel comfortable without it. Strutting amongst the bees and standing before Anna was different from being amidst so many plants with whom he hadn't had contact in twenty years.

Anna lay still, her mouth partly open, facing his side of the bed, the pages of a book splayed out in her hand. It was the same book she was always reading, a dog-eared copy with a woman wilting in the arms of a massive, bare-chested man on the cover. The couple was indoors but their hair swirled about them. Hedge assumed there must be a problem with the heating and air-conditioning system, which no doubt served as the mechanism that drove the plot forward. *Oh, Susanna!* it was called, and for some reason the title made Hedge's nose wrinkle in revulsion. But her place in the book was the same as it had been for quite some time, as though she hadn't been reading it. Why not? Why else would she lie awake with him?

He would miss figuring these puzzles. In fact, there were a great deal of things he would miss. Watching soapy shower water spiral down the drain; feeling the prickle of bees crawling over his face in search of pollen; Anna gripping his arm when she was alarmed. The things which fascinated him and made him feel needed.

Hedge leaned over, shut the book and set it on the nightstand. Then he returned to the foot of the bed, held out the toaster and pressed the lever down. The toaster made no sound, giving no indication that it was connecting two places separated by vast reaches of empty space. It simply rested in his hands while Hedge stared intently at Anna, wondering what she might be doing if not reading a book. It occurred to him that maybe reading a book was just another excuse to spend a few more waking moments with him in contemplative silence. It was nice not having to fill every instant with her in meaningless dialogue and pleasant to know that she could be comfortable and happy without having to do anything at all. Funny it took so long, and the prospect of being parted, to recognize details he had overlooked before.

Hedge began to smile when the lever popped up with a snap, the air turned electric, causing a few errant hairs to stand up on his head, then there was a quick sucking pop and Hedge disappeared in a soft flash as though he had quietly imploded.

All that remained as evidence he had been there were two indentations in the carpet where he stood, the shoes he had left at the foot of the bed, and a faint, lingering aroma of burnt bread.

PLANET PLANT

Hedge stood barefoot in the dirt, sopping wet and elbow to elbow with other agents who waited in silence for their turn to speak with the Council of Plants, facing the doors that led into the great chamber in orderly rows like stalks of corn. No one spoke, nor offered any chit chat, nor regaled one another with tales of their time amongst the humans because banter was tedious and served no purpose other than to waste time.

Hedge's teeth chattered in the quiet.

There were no tiled floors or soft carpeting in the waiting area outside the chamber. No comfortable chairs. No soothing music. No tedious magazines. Not a single triviality to pass the time. Strange how he had never truly understood the notion of Wasted Time until he stood here, dripping, with absolutely no means of wasting it.

He thought he'd wasted time with Anna, watching the glamorized violence on the television; wasted time sitting on the porch as he waited for the magical moment when the sunlight fell behind the willow and exploded it with radiant orange; wasted time gazing at Anna while the toaster buzzed in his hand before slinging him across the cosmos to end up standing here—in the mud, dripping wet, waiting indefinitely. The only wasted time, he decided, was not the moments idled away in pursuit of foolish pleasure, but that period of empty time where you did absolutely nothing and the next foreseeable event loomed somewhere beyond the horizon.

This, Hedge felt, was an unprecedented waste of time.

The great Chamber of the Council of Plants resembled a greenhouse, albeit on a colossal scale—a glassy pyramid that appeared dark because it absorbed light, broke it into its most beneficial parts, and showered them upon those within. It was here where the Council of Plants passed their legislature over the universe, determining what planets were ready to be welcomed into the Federation, which planets needed environmental tweaking to foster the growth of plants, and where strategies were chosen for striking underdeveloped planets where plants were oppressed by the dominant species.

It was this planet, named planet Plant, where plants first achieved cognizance and became rulers of their world. From here they branched into the cosmos to observe and guide the development of other worlds. So it had been for eons and eons, and there was no reason to think it would not continue for eons more.

Hedge touched the shoulder of the agent in front of him. She turned, blank faced.

"Excuse me," Hedge whispered. "Do you know why we're here?"

Several agents turned toward him, their expressions awestruck. Not all were human in appearance. Some were dogs, cats, or monkeys, while a great majority were plants.

The other agent stared at him a moment, then raised a finger to her mouth.

"Shhhhh."

Slowly, the other agents turned away.

They remained still, moving only when the great chamber doors swung ponderously apart, allowing one agent to exit while another was accepted, then ground together again with a regal boom. Though he strained and stretched whenever the doors opened there were far too many plants between Hedge and the chamber to see inside.

Hedge felt himself sinking into the dirt as he waited. On planet Plant there were no asphalt roads or cement causeways that led from one place to another, remained solid in rain, and gave the traveler a sense of direction and purpose based on a belief that all they need do to meet their goal was follow the path to its end. On planet Plant there was simply dirt because plants needed little else. Plants didn't move often, settling in one spot and remaining there, unchanged, for the majority of their existence. The whole of planet Plant, except where administrative structures stood and the great garden where the Plant of Ultimate Knowing resided, was covered by soft dirt mixed with dead leaves, wood chips, and decaying organic material. It smelled like old cabbage and squeezed between his toes and underneath the nails.

Planet Plant, Hedge thought, jaws clattering, toes flexing in the muck, was disgusting.

One might have expected planet Plant to be a glorious and verdant environment, the pinnacle of plant civilization, full of color and aroma, but that was not the case. Not by human standards, who lavished their capitals with adornments and whose rulers historically surrounded themselves with fineries that suited their notions of paradise—gardens and temples and statues and monuments and sports arenas—so other civilizations might look upon them with awed and envious eyes, and secretly wish they could share in the wonders of such a kingdom.

On planet Plant plants had no time to cultivate beauty. No time for plants to stop and simply grow as they did on the human planet. No time to celebrate their achievements by making their planet wonderful. Planet Plant was largely brown, and from far above had the appearance of a very old, worn penny.

Hedge shivered and shook, wringing a few drops of water from his heavy flannel shirt.

Every so often a series of thin black devices like toadstools rose from the sod, gurgled and burped hollowly, then sent out a thick mist of cold water. The chill water kept the dirt moist, serving as a medium through which nutrients could travel.

Clothing, Hedge observed, worked just like dirt, soaking up water and holding it in place so nutrients could move from here to there within the cotton fibers. Of course, clothing didn't need nutrients or water. Clothing didn't have growing parts like leaves or fruit. What clothing did was become clingy and unpleasant when filled with water, and water was cold, which made Hedge's teeth chatter. Clothing wasn't to blame. It was just obeying a law of physics Hedge didn't understand.

A human, on the other hand, knew better.

Humans always made coincidences and random misfortune out to be clever conspiracies. They not only gave inanimate objects the ability to reason and act, fascinated by the fantastic possibility that everything was imbued with a spirit and motivation, but often made the assumption that these inanimate objects were aware of their detrimental effect on the world around them, and worst of all, they were doing these things on purpose.

Anna had once stubbed her toe on the staircase as she carried laundry to their bedroom and fell forward in a heap. She cursed and writhed, clutching her foot as the clothing unfolded itself and slouched back down the staircase, then pounded on the carpeted steps to punish them for tripping her.

So it was strange, Hedge noted, that he was standing here, wet and uncomfortable, trying in very human fashion to guess what purpose his clothing had for soaking up water, and contemplating the possibility that it was just trying to be mean. Which was, of course, ridiculous.

Other agents who decided the wet clothing was a burden had simply removed it.

Hedge sighed, shifting in the disgusting dirt. He wanted desperately to rinse his feet and don a pair of shoes. That, too, struck him as strange.

He was a plant, so it made perfect sense to be standing in enriched dirt, soaking up nutrients of a potency that did not exist on the human planet. It should have been gloriously intoxicating. Yet this felt strange, maybe because it had been so long since he'd done it. He felt unusual doing this rather than the inefficient human means of nutrient uptake to which he'd grown accustomed. Even though much of what he took in through his mouth was placed in a storage vacuole for later disposal, there was a kind of pleasure in the act of eating, of feeling the textures of certain food and savoring their aroma. Many humans took great pleasure in eating, which was undoubtedly why so many of them grew to be very cumbersome and large.

Tentatively, Hedge bent and scooped up a handful of the cold, wet sod and put it in his mouth. He chewed.

Grainy, bitter, and foul. Hedge spat it out. Several plants regarded him with annoyance at the sound and the plant ahead of him turned again, raised a finger to her lips, then turned back. Hedge wiped his face and tried to avoid their gazes. He couldn't look down. Dirt was disgusting. So all that remained was up.

The night was thick and starry, the tiny white dots packed tightly against one another. The more he stared, the more he saw. Gradually he became aware of dimmer stars hovering beyond the more dominant ones, then still dimmer ones behind those as if he were peeling back layer after layer until he would at last reach the magnificent center of a great and profound onion.

Humanity called it space. Outer space. That's exactly what space was. The empty distance between objects. It was nothing. Yet it was a palpable nothing because it prevented those things that wanted to be together from being so.

The slow groan of the great doors parting drew his attention away from the sky and Hedge saw a familiar face enter the lobby, eyes downcast. Broad across the chest with a square face and thick, caterpillar eyebrows. Still dressed in the red and black flannel shirt he'd been wearing days before. Seeing someone he recognized helped Hedge feel more at ease.

"I saw you on the television a few days ago," said Hedge as the figure came close.

John Elm stopped and looked at Hedge, eyes glazed, face twisted by lingering confusion.

"Yeah," he answered distantly. Then, after a moment of thought added, "Yeah."

"Almost told them everything, eh?"

Hedge chuckled to himself, recalling how close they had come to disaster.

"Guess so," John replied. He puffed his cheeks and exhaled. "Don't much matter now, though, what bein' they're gonna destroy the place."

"Oh, really?"

For an instant Hedge didn't understand. Destroy the ShopMart selling the toasters? The parking lot where John had been interviewed? None of that made any sense. A moment passed before Hedge realized John was telling him, with an air of disappointment, that the Council intended to destroy the entire planet.

"Yeah," said John. "Really."

Hedge controlled himself. There was no need for alarm. This was a ruling issued by the Council of Plants, and thus a ruling that need not be questioned. But inside he could feel something winding up. Hedge became fidgety and restless, and his eyes darted here and there—at the listless agents around him, at the great doors from which issued a sense of complete indifference, at the space overhead in which planet Plant bobbed and rolled like an empty barrel, drifting out with the tide as the universe expanded and taking him further from the place he'd called home for twenty years.

His mind spun aimlessly, images of the place he remembered sweeping up and away so quickly he could only register a sense of desperation and loss. Impossible. Inexplicable. This was far worse than he suspected. In fact, he could think of no way to make the situation any more dismal.

As if in response, a black rod extended from the ground beside him, gurgled, and sent out a shower of chill water.

"Th-th-th-is is t-t-t-terrible," Hedge mumbled through chattering teeth. His gaze was intense but empty. All he could see was Anna's open and innocent expression as it gazed up into the sky, fascinated as the first rainbow waves of beautiful ruin fell upon humanity.

"Too bad," John agreed. He puffed at the water running down his face, then wiped it away with a sleeve. "Kinda liked it there. Oh well." He shrugged, began to shuffle away, then stopped. He came back to Hedge, whose astonishment was absolute. "Say," he added. "Did you have trouble with the safety valve phrase? My earth children insisted they didn't have an uncle Edwin."

THE CHAMBER OF THE COUNCIL OF PLANTS

It was bright inside the chamber of the Council of Plants. Not blinding, but a brightness that squeezed shadows to faint pencil lines. Hedge stood on the central platform at the base of the chamber where hundreds of plants looked down on him from tiered levels that rose to the acme of the pyramid. Those who stood where Hedge stood now often had the uncomfortable sense of being a germ looking up the shaft of a great microscope.

The council members looking down on him took in every detail, from his muddy, drenched clothing, to his fat, almost hairless body. Had Hedge been looking at them, he might have picked out the details of the council members as well. Some were as large as rainforest trees with wide canopies and trunks encased in thick stockings of knitted ivy cords while others appeared to be no more than stooped flower stalks topped by a few feathery petals.

But Hedge did not look around. Nor did he speak, or respond to questions, or make any outward motion. Instead, he stood before the Council, jaw canted and open, stunned speechless. Not by the impressive chamber or by the weight of so many eyes upon him. These things teetered at the rear of his mind, small and distant, waving frantically for fear of falling overboard and being lost in the wake of other thoughts.

Hedge didn't see the council plants. He'd already forgotten where he was. Forgotten his responsibilities to his species. His mind had been set adrift by the information given him by John Elm. Thinking of Anna and Scud and the bees and the squeaky hinge on the screen door and the disturbing hum-brrzap! of the bug lamp keeping him up at night and where to fit more pork chops and the mortifying thought that very soon all these trivialities would soon be rendered irrelevant.

He was so lost in thought that he didn't hear the Council's questions until they addressed him a third time.

"Agent Hedge!"

Hedge jolted. He was back in the chamber, dripping, feet caked with mud, shivering. The great majority of plants in this chamber lacked eyes, but it was clear their attention was focused upon him. Hedge blinked, wondering how long he'd been standing there.

"Yes?"

"I am pleased to have your attention," said a plant on the lowest tier. The plant was a gathering of long, mossy tendrils that draped over an ivory tabletop encircling the room. "My name is Chairplant Gulliver Stingfruit. I would like you to describe your observations of humanity. What do you make of them?"

A metal bar protruded before the plant, which Hedge supposed amplified the plant's voice and carried it through the chamber. While many plants could develop vocal cords, lungs, and various apparatuses to shape passing air into discernable sounds, many plants chose to remain true to their origins since all of plant society was based upon maintaining the *status quo*. Plants were rooted to the ground, immobile and, barring seasonal alterations, unchanging. Nothing required change, unless something strayed from the pattern plants had established, and then only to return it to the pattern. Which was why humanity had first come under scrutiny. They were a species of numerous social and political constants, such as discord and war, but were nevertheless constantly in flux so far as their technology and ambition was concerned.

The Council was silent, patiently awaiting his response.

His mouth opened. It wasn't until Hedge resigned himself to speak that he realized he wasn't sure what to say. Had he done his job? Had he observed humanity as he was supposed to? The majority of the time he'd spent working on various household chores, speaking with Scud Peabody at the diner, and watching the television with Anna. He should have been probing and infiltrating and discovering the dirty dark secrets which humanity kept buried in shoeboxes under the flowers and great vaults deep within their insidious institutions. Unfortunately, he'd never gotten around to it.

"Humans are very, ah, busy," Hedge began. He shivered. "With various projects. Space travel, thermodynamics, fission reactions, physics, horticulture. I, for example, cultivated an agricultural domain that produced food and other wares for carbon dioxide producing organisms, thus promoting the continuation of the life cycle on..."

"We are not interested in your activities and efforts to impersonate humans, agent Hedge," another plant interjected, "but the activities of the humans you observed. We do not deign to be human, we only emulate them to lull them into a false sense of security and thus learn their true nature. What are their ambitions? How do they plan to achieve them? Do they have any long-range plans for their race? Do those plans extend beyond their own planet? Are they benevolent or malevolent? Do they seek knowledge or dominion?"

Hedge cleared his throat.

"To be a better human is to better understand them, don't you think?"

A heavy silence fell. The idea of being human for any reason was surely distasteful. That all the plants here were restricted to flowerpots or the dirt to which they were rooted seemed to be evidence of that. There wasn't much purpose for a plant to move around, but Hedge couldn't bear the thought of being restricted to a vase or a patch of dirt having experienced the limited mobility that allowed him to travel to any dirt he chose.

Hedge detected this urge to argue and realized it was one of many human traits he had acquired in his time amongst them.

"This is an example of what humans refer to as Flippancy," Hedge said quickly. "They are a very sarcastic species, and for this reason it is sometimes difficult to understand what they mean because often, such as when they are being flippant, they mean just the opposite of what they say."

"A telling piece of information," said Stingfruit gruffly. "Please answer the question."

"Because my location was largely rural I did not come into contact with a great many humans."

"Then what of those you *did* meet? What was your understanding of them?"

Hedge thought of the diner and the vindictive Garry Thorne, how they swarmed upon Scud like fire ants. He thought of the television, always spewing doom and frightening Anna. Hedge's experiences could easily serve as encapsulated encounters with the whole of humanity. They were nasty and dangerous. Yet Hedge could not bring himself to tell the Council such a stark and brutal truth.

"They did not appear to have any plans for galactic conquest," Hedge answered. That, at least, was true. Humanity was largely decentralized. They joined together in factions, but hadn't mustered their collective might, and thus their achievements were muted. "However, I am sure there is much more to learn and would be glad of the opportunity to continue in this role."

There were murmurs and grumbles from the Council as they conferred with one another. Stingfruit spoke again.

"Yes," he said. "A sentiment shared by a number of your peers."

"Indeed," agreed another. "It is a most suspicious phenomenon, this desire to return. One that cannot help but make us wonder if the humans have infiltrated our system of spies in order to save their species from certain ruin. A ruin, I might add, they richly deserve. Perhaps a few humans are posing as plants that are posing as humans and intend to report to their masters. Foolish though they may be, there are quite a lot of them, so the probability is very high that one of them could insert themselves into our network by chance or design."

"Most like by chance," said another.

"Are you such a counterspy, agent Hedge?" asked Stingfruit.

It was probably because Hedge had spent so much slow time in the presence of humanity that the gravity of this question did not penetrate immediately. He stood several moments before realizing he was suspected not just of treason, which was stunning of its own accord, but of being human as well.

"Me? A counterspy? I don't think so. No, no. Of course not. Why should I wish to spy upon my own kind? We have done nothing worthy of scrutiny, have we? I just want to assist in the fashion that I am best able."

There was murmuring amongst the plants for a few moments before the chairplant spoke to him again.

"Very well, Hedge. While your prolonged exposure to humanity has clearly dulled your judgment and made you argumentative and *flippant*, as you say, we believe you."

"However," said still another, "though we appreciate your services, you will not be returning in such a capacity. Humanity has been deemed too reckless, and will be liquidated."

So it was true. Hedge felt his insides plummet.

"Liquidated? Why?"

"Humankind is not a pleasant race," explained the chairplant in a sighing, faintly agitated tone which made it seem as though it had done so several times before. "On a grand scale, their history is laced with war and social unrest. On a small scale they exhibit a general intolerance of one another, resulting in various levels of criminal behavior, including the murder of their own kind. This sort of behavior is unacceptably hypocritical for a species which deems itself sentient and civil. Behavior that we believe is a direct consequence of having forward-facing eyes."

Hedge wasn't certain he'd heard correctly.

"Forward-facing eyes?"

"Yes," said Stingfruit. "They simply cannot help themselves."

"I don't understand."

Another plant made a blustery, throat-clearing noise. It too was on the lowest level. A short, drooping tree no taller than Hedge, with foliage that reminded him of a thick, brushy mustache. It made another noise and Hedge saw its leaves flutter where the words passed. Certain it had the attention of the chamber, the plant spoke.

"It is a scientific fact that those creatures with forward-facing eyes use this feature to hunt prey, using the depth perception it permits them to pinpoint their lunges. Whereas those creatures without eyes, or with eyes on the sides of their head, are passive and use their panoramic vision to elude stalking predators who have forward-facing eyes. Those with eyes on the sides of their head consider their surroundings more thoroughly, while those with forward-facing eyes pick a target and plow blindly toward it, oblivious of how this approach disrupts their environment."

A much taller plant beside the mustache plant, with a long, pale trunk and a few sharp leaves at the top, continued.

"All they see are objectives and obstacles to be met or overcome or obliterated as they rumble forward in a straight line, over, under, or through. Nor do they ever see the havoc they leave in their wake, the forward-facing eyes fixed already upon their next objective. This aggression has led to recklessness in virtually every aspect of their society, playing a notable role in their technological progress. Reckless advancement is their most reliable method of discovery, learning more through accident than ingenuity, diving wildly forward in pursuit of success rather than taking stock of the effects their experiments have upon the world around them."

Here the chairplant resumed control of the argument.

"Their frequent use of thermonuclear devices and particle accelerators not just in times of war, but also experimentally out of lunatic curiosity, is extremely disturbing. They are not just a danger to themselves, or others, but to Everything. It is for that reason that we *must* intervene."

"There is only one solution," said a plant near the acme.

"We must protect the universe."

"One cannot trust those with forward-facing eyes."

The voices sounded from several places now as numerous plants added their input.

"It is our duty to every creature, every system, every grain of matter that we do so and do so thoroughly. When a branch dies, before it becomes filled with insects or infection to poison the rest of the plant we cut it off. The universe itself is a plant. So it is with a species that poses a threat to the universe."

The blustery plant took up the speech again.

"We are not only going to have to eliminate humans, but also anything else that might evolve into one, including apes, cheetahs, whales, meerkats, kangaroos and koala bears."

When they were quiet again the chairplant spoke.

"You understand why we must do this. You were there. You should know best of all."

When Hedge considered, it was true. The majority of humanity was foul and unpleasant. Garry Thornes aplenty, filling diners and church pews alike. But what about the Scuds and Annas and other such rarities? Was it right to extinguish those few bright spots for the sins of the many? On the other hand, was it okay to spare all the foul corruptions for the sake of a few?

He understood the rationale behind eliminating humanity. It made perfect sense in his head. But his heart wasn't in agreement, which made little sense because Hedge did not have a heart and was governed by logic rather than blind emotion. It was a distinctly human notion, one of many Hedge found difficult to understand, because the brain was the dominant nerve mass in the human body, not the heart. The heart did not serve any role in the process of decision making, it merely pounded blood and sewage through miles of intricate piping. Still, he couldn't suppress this lingering sensation of doubt. He wasn't convinced this course of action was correct, and it bothered him that he didn't wholly agree with a Council which had governed the cosmos for ages uncounted.

His mind raced in search of images in their defense. A flash of inspiration or a courtesy paid to plant life by humanity. Maybe they weren't fully understood. He had to save them so they could be further studied. Had to save them so he could get back because it didn't feel right here, didn't feel natural. It occurred to Hedge that plant though he may be, he was not like the others, there was really only one place where he belonged, and soon it would be gone.

For whatever reason his mind flashed with the image of those silly people in the diner, not speaking to one another, but gathered at the counter, still faces fixed on a tiny black and white television while men in body armor ran about in formations, fighting over a wedge of rubber called a football. Hedge could scarcely tell who was who or what they were trying to do on the tiny screen, but every so often there would be a great cheer or a sigh of utter despair.

Sports befuddled him.

"We can't," Hedge blurted.

"Can't what?" asked a plant from somewhere behind Hedge. "We can do anything."

"Shouldn't, then," he responded, and looked around the room to gauge the reaction.

Mumblings and sounds of general agitation rumbled through the chamber.

The tendrils of the chairplant tightened on the edge of the counter and pulled itself toward Hedge.

"Shouldn't *what?*" it asked in a daring tone.

"Shouldn't destroy them," Hedge clarified.

Until now it had seemed that many of the plants in this forum had allowed their attention to wander, speaking quietly to one another until this encounter was over. After all, they had already done this several hundred times over without a flutter. Now something was changed. Someone was challenging the decision of the Council, and Hedge felt the entire weight of the room shift to bear on him.

"Oh? For what reason should we allow them to go on? What purpose do they serve?"

The response had been instinctive, thoughtless. Now that it was done he could not take it back. But Hedge knew the human impulse often proved correct without knowing how or why, or having an immediately apparent reason. And because he knew he was right he was certain there must be a reason. All he needed to do was figure it out.

"Because I..."

At that moment he understood their silly obsession. Why they suffered when their team did poorly and exulted when it did well. It was an investment of hope and faith in something wholly beyond their control, and there was nothing so gratifying as having blind hope or silly faith rewarded with success because success was not guaranteed, but willed into being through the sheer force of devotion.

"... I want them to do well."

It was a bold, honest, and passionate statement. And, Hedge knew immediately, the wrong thing to say.

The chairplant settled back into its place.

"Yes. We have observed similar sympathies in others of your position."

Emotion was generally understood to get in the way of sound judgment. It delayed action when action was most necessary. Such as when Hedge had cornered a mouse in the living room that had been tearing out the stuffing of the living room couch and pooping on the kitchen countertop. He had paused for just an instant, considering the fact that this animal was simply existing in the only fashion it knew how, with no hint of the dismay it caused others. In that instant, while Hedge locked his gaze with the beady orbs of the insignificant rodent and considered the perspective of the tiny creature as it faced oblivion, it dashed away and was gone.

Yet Hedge had not regretted the hesitation. In fact, he felt relieved by its escape. He knew it was unlikely, but perhaps this brush with death would serve as cathartic moment for the mouse, at which point it would amend its ways and realize the strife it caused Hedge. The next morning, as per the routine, he found a handful of couch stuffing strewn across the living room floor and a liberal sprinkling of mouse pellets on the countertop.

"So, you understand, then?" he asked.

"Certainly," said the chairplant. "A universal flaw that will be corrected in future attempts to evaluate weaker cognizant species after the annihilation of humanity. That will be all, agent Hedge. You may leave. We will find a new role for you to play since there will be no use in emulating people. Until that time, enjoy the planet whence all plants derived."

Hedge's shoulders slouched. He had failed.

"No," interrupted a powerful voice from the council. When Hedge looked for the source he found it originated not from a single plant, but a clump of daisies growing from the rotten log of a fallen tree. Their many voices joined into a chorus that was both musical and commanding at the same time. "We have heard similar stories from a great many agents now. Perhaps this notion of sympathy has merit."

There was a rapid flurry of hushed discussion, flapping of branches and shaking of leaves as the plants argued, so involved with one another they made no attempt to communicate through the devices, and Hedge had no idea what was being said.

In one final flurry of sound punctuated by an orchestral blast of noise from the daisies the argument came to a close and there was a sudden silence and a few leaves danced through the air and settled beside Hedge.

Stingfruit seemed disgusted.

There was no facial expression Hedge could read, no mashed eyebrows or downward arcing scowl, but there was a certain air of defeat and indignation that wafted from the plant like the chilly mist which made him shiver when he pulled open the icebox.

"Very well," it grumbled. "We have conferred. We will not destroy humanity. They are a curious species full of innovation. Surely the empathy which has infected so many cannot be a fluke. Nor are humans clever enough to have inspired such... feeling... so deliberately. But they remain a danger that must be dealt with."

Hedge might have danced if he knew how and were his body suited for such activity. It was a strange, overwhelming sense of pure elation that built inside him like too many pork chops, and Hedge felt if he didn't release them he might burst. This was a new sensation for Hedge and because of his inexperience he had no idea how to release the pent up energy. All he could do was emulate the fashion in which he had seen humans expressing their most extreme joy, eyes welling as emotion overrode their brains.

Hedge straightened, stretched both arms into the air above him and balanced on his toes. A single word rang from him and crashed against the contemplative silence of the chamber.

"Touchdown!" he cried.

All was quiet in the chamber as the echoing shout bounced up and down through the room, slowly expending its energy like the funny ball that hopped erratically on the playing field before coming to rest beneath a heap of bodies.

The pause continued until Hedge's elation waned and he began to feel self-conscious about the outburst, knowing they didn't understand and should they ask he would not be able to explain it to them.

Mercifully, rather than inquire, the daisies took over the dialogue.

"Rather than eliminate them and repopulate their planet, we will send a task force to store them. You will be part of this task force, since your passion for them has clearly reached a crescendo that transcends understanding. We are certain your interest will ensure that nothing goes awry."

The joy and relief of victory was extremely brief.

Storage! That was little more than eternal imprisonment, locked in stasis in the great vaults where various odds and ends the plant Council found potentially useful or briefly fanciful until they were forgotten.

"But..."

"There will be no more argument," said the daisies. "Our flexibility has limits. We have given you as much opportunity as we were able. An intelligent agent will make the best of this new opportunity."

True. He had certainly pushed his luck as far as it would go. There had to be another solution. But what?

There was only one thing to do when one required answers beyond their own reckoning: consult the Plant of Ultimate Knowing.

FORKED

Scud knew the visitor was different from the moment he stumped through the door with a crooked smile on his face and a toaster in his hands. He had an air of mystery and deception about him, just like Hedge. The visitor must have sensed his understanding because he made straight for Scud, even as he emptied the dirty dishes from an abandoned table.

"Hello. My name is Mr. Visitor."

"Hello, Mr. V… V… Mr. V…" Scud sighed. "Hello."

"I was wondering if you could help me. I'm looking for someone… unique."

Scud's eyes flicked toward a corner booth where Garry Thorne suddenly perked.

"You'll want M… Mr. Hedge, then, s… sir," he whispered.

"Look at that!" shouted Garry Thorne from the corner of the diner. "If old Scud ain't the most popular shithead in town!"

"Tell me about Mr. Hedge. What makes him unique?"

Behind the visitor, Garry had risen from his seat. Scud clutched the bin of dirty dishes tighter.

"I'm n… not sure I should t… tell you. You m…might be dangerous. Are you dangerous?"

"Extremely," said Mr. Visitor. "However, to not provide me with the information I require would be equally dangerous. Not just for yourself, but everyone here. Everyone everywhere."

Garry approached them, fishing for a pack of cigarettes in his breast pocket.

Scud spoke in a hurried whisper, anxious to be free of this attention. Things generally went badly for him when he was the subject of attention.

"He's from another p… planet, for one. And he's a p… plant. You should g… g… go."

"Go? Is that all?"

Garry stepped up beside Mr. Visitor, an unlit cigarette hanging from his mouth.

"Yeah, Scud. Can'tcha see this fella wants to talk with ya? Prolly cause you're so cute!"

Mr. Visitor turned to face Garry.

"I understand you are trying to be of assistance, but your skills in discourse are painfully lacking. Please return to your seat where you will be less distracting."

Garry stiffened, then jabbed a finger into Mr. Visitor's chest. Mr. Visitor looked down at the finger in fascination.

"What did you say, you shiny piece of fuck?"

Mr. Visitor regarded Garry with an expression of bemusement.

"The first part of your question seems rhetorical. My proximity and volume are such that you should have no trouble hearing. The only remaining explanations are that your hearing has been impaired or that you are a fool. Your vocal pitch may be a symptom of impairment. I will attempt the message at a higher volume. YOU ARE A DISTRACTION. DISTRACTION IS WITHOUT VALUE. YOUR EXISTENCE IS THEREFORE, BY ASSOCIATION, WITHOUT VALUE. THIS IS A BASIC MATHEMATICAL PRINCIPLE YOU SHOULD UNDERSTAND UNLESS YOU ARE A FOOL. ARE YOU A FOOL? PLEASE OFFER SOME SIGN THAT YOU COMPREHEND OR I MUST CONCLUDE YOUR STUPIDITY IS ABSOLUTE."

Garry's face had gone entirely red as Mr. Visitor spoke. When he finished, Garry snatched a fork from the table and brandished it before Mr. Visitor.

"I am going to fuck your goddamn eyes out!"

Garry reared back and drove the fork into Mr. Visitor's cheek. The tines sank in up to the handle. To Scud's surprise, no blood came out and Mr. Visitor's expression did not change. Judging by the way the redness drained out of Garry's face, he must have been surprised as well. Mr. Visitor batted Garry's hand away, the fork still lodged in his wooden face, then turned to Scud.

"This human does not appear to have a properly functioning mind. Please wait here. I will be only a moment."

Mr. Visitor turned abruptly away again to Garry, who stood his ground, though he was visibly shaken by the fact that his blow had had no effect. His eyes were wide and his legs wobbled beneath him.

"What the hell are you?" asked Garry.

"A messenger," said Mr. Visitor, striding toward Garry. Mr. Visitor's voice did not change volume, but it reverberated nevertheless. "I am a harbinger of destruction. You should return to those you cherish in anticipation of annihilation, unless you prefer that I render you unto oblivion now. Broken-minded fool though you may be, I will permit you this choice."

As he spoke, he stepped toward Garry, who stood his ground until the two met. Mr. Visitor moved forward inexorably, like an avalanche in slow motion, and Garry was forced to give ground. Garry watched the fork waggle as Mr. Visitor spoke to him, all the while being herded toward the exit.

"It is my wish that you depart. You will depart and allow me to proceed. My will shall be realized for it is greater than yours. You will depart and grasp the significance of my being here when I am urgently needed over there, and how this distraction rankles me. Your efforts to unhinge and oppress do your species a great disservice at a critical moment. You shall not be missed should you suffer obliteration."

With the conclusion of this speech, Garry's back met the door and it swung open behind him.

Garry gave Mr. Visitor a long, withering look that he shifted briefly to Scud. He pushed a potted plant off its perch by the entrance in a final act of unprovoked malevolence, spit a thick wad at his feet, then left.

Satisfied, Mr. Visitor turned on his heel and stood before Scud.

"Thank you for h… helping me," said Scud.

"Nevermind that," said Mr. Visitor, the fork bobbing up and down as he spoke. "You must help me before I can truly help you."

Scud didn't pay much attention to what Mr. Visitor was saying, distracted by the waggling fork. Odd that Mr. Visitor was so strongly opposed to distraction, yet didn't notice the fork hanging out of his cheek. Without thinking, Scud reached up and pulled on the handle. The fork slid out with ease and Scud dropped the utensil into the bin of soapy water with the other silverware.

"Thank you," said Mr. Visitor. He paused to massage the holes in his cheek. When he had finished they were gone. "Now. Where can I find Mr. Hedge?"

IN THE GARDEN OF THE PLANT OF ULTIMATE KNOWING

The garden where the Plant of Ultimate Knowing dwelled was immense, with massive clumps of flowers and shrubs growing in great bumps, and trees gathered in tight buttes, all rolling into the distance like the rumpled surface of a shoreless ocean. Each time Hedge thought he'd figured out where the garden ended he saw a faint bit of motion from an acolyte moving on a faraway crest. It was like trying to detect the far wall of the infinite sky, or tracking down the source of a rainbow—each time he thought he had it, it would take another step out of reach.

Hedge followed a weaving path of stiff vines through the boundless garden, toaster in hand. There was a lump of building not far away and, as the only structure in view, it seemed logical to assume he would find the great Plant there.

Numerous acolytes wandered through the garden, mobile forms of plants that tilled the dirt and squirted the grounds with water. They appeared unaware of Hedge, which was all right with him. A human might stop and stare, then mumble a few disapproving words to an associate. It wasn't malicious. They were naturally suspicious and careful about the disruption of their comfortable, familiar environment.

The trip here required little alteration to the toaster. Just a slight turn on a screw with his thumbnail to realign where he was with where he was going, a quick jolt like the jerk from a dog reaching the end of its lead, then he was here, ears faintly jangling as though he'd brushed the porch windchime, the aroma of burnt bread in his nose.

He could very well have transported himself directly into the presence of the great Plant, but, quite frankly, Hedge had no idea where the Plant was or what it looked like.

In truth no one seemed to know much about the Plant of Ultimate Knowing. They knew it was ancient and omniscient, but outside of knowing it resided in the great garden on planet Plant, nothing. Not what it looked like, not where it came from, not even the last remarkable statement it had made. The notorious Plant was shrouded in mystique, straddling the boundary between reality and mythology like Confucius or Buddha or Jesus. The idea of the great Plant was so close to perfect it filled the faithful with hope and left the cynical groping for truth. Everyone had heard of it, everyone knew its counsel was sought in times of great indecision, but no one seemed to have met it.

At least puzzling through the mystery of the Plant's location allowed the enormity of what he was doing to build slowly rather than crash upon him in a quick, thundering smash. Searching for the Plant would provide time to gather his thoughts, determine how best to phrase his question, and most importantly, give him time enough to come to his senses and reconsider.

Speaking with the Plant on this subject could easily be considered treason and he hoped the Plant of Ultimate Knowing would either sympathize with the plight of humanity and explain how Hedge could save them, or at the very least convince him the Council was right. It was the great Plant of Ultimate Knowing that suggested they study humanity in the first place.

If it had to be the latter, and Hedge suspected it would be, he hoped the Plant would be kind enough to satisfy itself with the knowledge that it had turned Hedge away from disaster rather than tell the Council his aim in coming here. It was these hopes that pressed him forward.

There had been only one plant in history convicted of treason. A plant for whom history had no name. All that remained to commemorate the ignominious existence of the traitor plant was its unthinkable and mortifying crime, which rang through history as clearly as a church bell calling the penitent to its door on a solemn Sunday morning. This plant had attempted to blow up the Council, insisting plants had no right to dictate the existences of other species. The plant was captured, put on trial, and sentenced to be mulched.

Hedge shuddered.

Mulched. How horrific. Moreso when he thought he too may share such a fate. Become nameless and reviled by an entire species. And not so long ago the largest of his worries was the consumption of a few pork chops. How he missed that distant world more than ever.

Hedge passed through the vaulted aperture in the front of what Hedge had thought a building from a distance, but could see now that it was actually a heaping of crawling vines shaped into a dome. It encased a broad area with the imperfect grip of an overturned colander, allowing bands of light to slip through in thousands of humming strands.

He felt himself shaking with the understanding that he would soon be in the presence of an awesome creature whose existence spanned eons. Its knowledge penetrated everything: physics, chemistry, botany, philosophy. There were rumors it could see through time, and certainly it could read Hedge's thoughts as plainly as Hedge could read roadside billboards: 3 miles to next Rest Stop; 5 miles to next Act of Insubordination and Treason.

The thought that all his secrets would be laid bare in such stark fashion frightened him. Not just because they were his private thoughts which no one should know, but because of the realization that he had secrets when, as an honest and open plant, he shouldn't. The Plant of Ultimate Knowing would see he cared entirely too much for the humans and judge they had turned him from his true purpose. Or worse, it would delve into his mind and learn the Council was right, that Hedge was a human interloper trying to save his kinsmen, even though that wasn't entirely true. There was only evidence enough to support its trueness.

It had been a mistake to come here, Hedge realized. The visit would only bring disaster. The Council may be wrong, but Hedge lacked the evidence and intellect to turn them from such a course.

He turned back down the path but found his way blocked by the towering form of a garden acolyte as it moved toward him. The foliage on either side was too thick to press through without damaging it. The acolyte had no eyes, no face, only a thick green trunk with a great gathering of tendrils at the base that writhed slowly like an octopus flexing faintly to keep itself level in the water. It did not attempt to care for any of the plants on either side of the path, it simply remained, too large to go around.

Hedge would have to find a different way out.

He resumed following the path and after a few steps his heel sank into soft dirt. At first he thought he'd gone off the path, but soon realized he'd wandered into a cloister of some sort where several of the paths converged and the soil was rich and black. Unlike the rest of the garden, this patch was absent of plantlife but for a solitary fat stalk as big around as his head that thrust out of the ground.

The stalk arced high over Hedge and his neck craned back to take in the rest of the plant. A single leaf curled away from the trunk like the peel of a partially opened banana, and the top was dominated by the huge, brown-budded face of an enormous sunflower that hung over him like a dormant showerhead: the Plant of Ultimate Knowing.

Light and fast as he was able, Hedge made for the nearest open path. As he approached, another acolyte stepped out of the growth and stopped on the path, filling it. He moved toward the next, but an acolyte was already emerging. As he looked around the clearing he saw that all the paths had been filled by silent watchmen. There was no way out.

Hedge fumbled with the toaster.

WHY HAVE YOU COME?
The voice boomed through the garden, slow and powerful like a rhinoceros plowing through the soft husks of dead trees, emanating from everywhere and hammering Hedge's mind with thundering boldface. Startled, the toaster fell out of his hands.

Hedge knew he was trapped. The plant was surely already peering into his mind, reading the long scroll of his thoughts as they unspooled from the typewriter: Run, Hide, Anna, Bees. Full of mortification and despair, pity and frustration.

He opened his mouth to respond, stooping for the toaster as he searched for the proper words to use for a creature who had been extant for so many eons, realizing banter and trite speak would be tiresome and that he should just get right to the point. Then paused.

Something was amiss.

The domed enclosure was appropriately arcane and awe inspiring, the air stank of a moldy, sodden swamp. Bees hummed in majestic monotone as they moved from plant to plant, giving the dome a pastoral air that reminded Hedge of earth-home, his ears filled with the sound of a choir that could sing just one note, but performed it with soul-stirring flawlessness. Everything seemed fitting. With exception, he decided, to the Plant of Ultimate Knowing. There was something overblown and conspicuous about the copious amount of detritus and mood. There was too much *atmosphere*. It was what humans called a Contrivance, where the situation was arranged to generate a preordained opinion. This, the cavernous room, the abundance of plantlife, the size of the Plant of Ultimate Knowing, was designed to create Awe.

Hedge knew it was the negative influence of humanity which brought him to this suspicious conclusion but couldn't resist the impulse to see this line of thought through to the end.

Contrivance was a clever way of saying Lie, and Lie was deception. Deception was intended to take one from the course of truth, and it was the deception that troubled Hedge. Why would he be led from truth and what was the truth that was being hidden from him?

The problem wasn't so much with the chamber, but that the Plant of Ultimate Knowing didn't belong in it. If the plant was indeed all knowing it would not only know the question but have an answer prepared. Couldn't the plant see his thoughts? Extrapolate his reasons for being here simply through the tilt in his gait, or the slant of his brow or the timbre of his voice? It was the Plant of *Ultimate* Knowing after all, not the Plant of *Mostly* Knowing or the Plant of *Kind of Guessing*.

So instead of presenting his question to the Plant in a humble fashion as was befitting a plant of its prestige, Hedge found himself being what most humans tended to be when they were in a situation where they were disadvantaged or dubious: Impertinent.

"Aren't you the Plant of Ultimate Knowing? Shouldn't you know why I'm here?"

The Plant was unfazed.

IT WAS A RHETORICAL QUESTION

Still, Hedge was suspicious.

"So?" asked Hedge.

SO, WHAT? the Plant replied.

"If you know why I'm here, provide me with a solution."

There was a pause, a low rumbling as though the plant were muttering to itself, then its voice regained its imperious volume.

IT IS TRADITIONAL TO FORMALLY VOICE YOUR QUESTION TO THE PLANT OF ULTIMATE KNOWING

Oh.

"I have been asked by the Council to place humanity in storage, which will essentially end their civilization. I know I should simply obey, but there is something intangible, a sense of discomfort in this solution, that tells me the Council may be in error. Surely humanity is wretched and miserable and antagonistic, but their good features at the very least equal their bad. They care for their elderly..."

ONLY IN THE HOPE THAT THEY WILL BE CARED FOR WHEN THEY ARE ELDERLY. IT IS MERELY ROUNDABOUT SELFISHNESS. A WAY OF PERFORMING SO OTHERS MIGHT DUPLICATE WHAT THEY DEEM KINDNESS. THEY ARE APES, AFTER ALL, WHO LEARN THROUGH IMITATION

"But there are many other examples of their altruism that are undertaken simply to content themselves with the knowledge that they have done what is Right. Surely no species that seeks Rightness, in spite of their frequent inability to find it, is worth eradication. Is there an alternate solution to propose to the Council? What is that proposal and how do I get it to them? What must I do?"

The Plant pondered for a moment, as though considering the question, which seemed unnecessary, again, because it was a plant of Ultimate Knowing. There really shouldn't be a process, just an answer. This was very strange.

The long stalk began to stoop, bending in thought or trying to listen to a very quiet voice over the steady drone of the bees.

"Hey," called a small voice from behind Hedge.

He looked back to a row of bushes running along the edge of the enclosure where it seemed the voice originated, but saw nothing. An acolyte stood nearby, silent and still.

There was a creaking sound as of an old, oaken door straining on its hinges. The great Plant was straightening. It had his answer.

YOU ASK WHAT YOU MUST DO. THE ANSWER IS, YOU MUST DO NOTHING

"What? Why?"

YOU MUST DO AS YOU ARE FATED. AS I GAZE INTO YOUR FUTURE I SEE YOUR FATE IS TO DO NOTHING. DOING OTHER THAN NOTHING WILL ONLY GET IN THE WAY OF FATE, WHICH CANNOT BE GOTTEN IN THE WAY OF, AND THUS YOU WOULD EXHAUST YOURSELF NEEDLESSLY. NOTHING IS ALL THAT YOU CAN DO BECAUSE IT IS ALL THAT YOU SHALL ACCOMPLISH

"But if we are all pulled along by fate and no one acts, how does anything happen?"

NO ONE ACTS UNLESS THEY ARE FATED TO ACT, THUS FATE ACTS THROUGH THEM. YOU MUST ONLY ACT IF YOU ARE FATED TO DO SO

Hedge's mind spun as he tried to follow the tangle of words.

"How am I supposed to know if I'm fated to act?"

YOU WILL SIMPLY ACT

"But how do I know that's fate, and not my decision? How do I distinguish when I am complying with fate from when I am getting in its way?"

THERE ARE NO DECISIONS IN FATE. ONLY ACTIONS WHICH ARE FATED

It was possible, being this was a Plant of Ultimate Knowing, that this logic made perfect sense to all-knowing plants who spent all their time in deep and important thought. At the same time, were a plant so all-knowing, it would seem obvious to such an intelligent plant that Hedge had no idea what the Plant was trying to tell him and would attempt to explain in much simpler terms.

Since this did not appear to be the case, Hedge felt compelled to express his confusion in the way most humans expressed themselves when they did not understand something.

"What?"

THERE IS NO MORE I NEED SAY

With that the Plant of Ultimate Knowing began to sag, retreating into thought or slumber, and it was clear the Plant would have no more to do with him.

Hedge felt heavy on the inside, though he'd not eaten anything but the mouthful of dirt outside the Council chamber in the past two days. The Plant had not met any of his hopes, neither posing a different plan to save humanity, nor justifying the Council's decision. Suffice to say, Hedge was extremely disappointed and distraught to discover the most ancient Plant in all the cosmos, known for its wisdom and knowledge, was either unwilling to help, or more worrisome still, did not know how.

"Hey!"

Again the voice came from the bushes, more insistent this time, so Hedge made his way toward them through the soft dirt of the clearing. He searched about for the source of the voice, pulling apart branches, glancing up at the stoic acolyte in suspicion, then turning in place to scan his surroundings. All he saw was more acolytes, flitting black specks of bees and the useless Plant of Ultimate Knowing.

"I know why the decision disturbs you."

This time Hedge was certain the voice came from the bushes, but still couldn't see where.

"Down here."

Below the bushes, hidden beneath thick, scratchy branches and thumbnail leaves, was a small, rudimentary plant no larger than Hedge's outstretched hand. Two small red leaves stood at the acme of a threadlike stem—a simple weed. Was this the plant speaking to him? He lay down on his stomach and poked the weed with a finger.

"Stop that," said the weed, annoyed.

"Why does the decision disturb me?" asked Hedge.

"Because you know it is fundamentally wrong," the weed explained. "You know it is wrong to decide the fate of an entire species, to cast a verdict of doom upon that which does not meet your approval, yet you have been brainwashed into obeying every command given you by the Council and endorsed by the Plant of Ultimate Knowing. Duped by a governing body who has manipulated the truth with the singular purpose of maintaining its iron grip upon the universe."

There was something greatly amiss with this weed. Very simple in appearance when compared the to far more complex plants and organisms growing around it, such as the acolytes and bees and much larger trees and bushes. Like the Plant of Ultimate Knowing, this weed too seemed greatly out of place, though in a much different fashion, and the difference fascinated him. It seemed to hearken back to a time long before the elaborations of evolution, to the earliest forms of plantlife.

"Who are you? What are you doing here?"

"Hiding."

Hedge's gaze darted around in suspicion, but there was no movement elsewhere. The acolytes were perfectly motionless and the great Plant was quiet, its knowledge spent.

"From what?" he whispered. "The Plant of Ultimate Knowing?"

"That empty, pedantic puppet?" sneered the red-leaved weed. "No. My past. When those preposterous dopes accused me of treason and sentenced me to be mulched."

Hedge took an involuntary gasp of air, sucking loose dirt into his throat and sending him into a fit of choked coughing.

"You... tried," Hedge coughed. "Blow up..." Cough, cough. "Blow up... Council? How are you here? You were destroyed!"

"I made no such attempt. A disgusting, filthy fabrication to sully my image. Fortunately, I eluded them and avoided destruction, though that didn't prevent them from spreading the lie. Destroying me would make it easier to insert their marionette into the role of Plant of Ultimate Knowing because they knew how important it was to have one. A Plant of Ultimate Knowing brings a very *religious* form of comfort. Someone is watching over us, is there to catch us when we fall, guide us back to the path should we go astray. Why fear anything if the almighty, in all their wisdom, condones your actions? Even better when it is they who make it dance."

Hedge's mind reeled. The flood of information pouring out of this weed was almost more than his mind could hold all at once, and, like the pork chops, he feared his brain might begin emptying other things out to make room for the new data.

The Plant of Ultimate Knowing was a false deity. The Council was concerned not for the welfare of the universe, but rather for its own survival. This weed...

"*You* are the Plant of Ultimate Knowing?"

The weed snorted.

"I was, though I wouldn't be so brash as to use such a title. I am the advisor the Council replaced when the advice no longer satisfied them. Now that towering abomination is my successor. Not that it knows anything at all. It's just a sock puppet."

"That was ages ago!"

"Was it? Hard to determine. Time doesn't appear to move so much when nothing moves around you. You scarcely even note its passing."

"You sound lonely."

A human might have shrugged, but the weed had no such option. It made a noise of indifference.

"Lonely, maybe. Mostly bored," it said. Then with more enthusiasm, "So! You've come here to save humanity. You must be Hedge."

Hedge's eyes flew open.

"You *are* prescient!"

"Horse hockey. Delve into the future? Know the unknowable? See the invisible? Those are silly canards invented to give weight to the spoutings of that insipid behemoth. One can formulate a guess, note the emergence of familiar patterns, but tell the future? Absurd. It's all about having information and knowing how to use it."

I KNOW ALL, I SEE ALL, I AM ALL called the giant sunflower drowsily from the center of the clearing.

"Blabbering windbag," the smaller plant muttered.

"Then how did you know who I was? Why I was here?"

"I just told you. Information. Knowledge is power. I still have friends and sympathizers in the Council. Surely you can guess who they are."

Hedge thought back to his experience in the Council chamber and a sense of tininess and insignificance took him. All the stern, authoritative voices and powerful minds. None seemed to be in his favor. All of them seemed to want humanity exterminated, with exception to the daisies. Strange how those daises, in the face of the entire Council, had swayed them to alter their decision. The daisies. Could it be them? What was it they had told him?

We have given you as much opportunity as we were able. An intelligent agent will make the best of this new opportunity.

"And these acolytes, friends who have kept me hidden, were kind enough to guide you to me. Even they were roused by your arguments, though a bit puzzled by your expressions of enthusiasm."

The acolyte beside him made no outward movement of acknowledgment.

"You heard that?"

"You want humanity to do well, do you?" asked the weed. "There's an idealistic statement if I ever heard one. Blind and foolish. Much like many of their philosophies. But... not without merit."

"The Council thinks humans might have infiltrated our system of spies." Hedge shook his head in wonder at the revelations to which he'd been subjected. "They think I might be one of them!"

"The consequence of a policy of deception is that the deceivers will invariably come to suspect they too are being deceived. By those they are deceiving and everyone else around them. Certainly an intelligent and observant agent such as yourself realizes that they are indeed becoming more human. But that isn't what really worries them."

"Then what?"

"Humanity has already reached this stage of development plants are now exhibiting. They suspect everyone. But that means, since they are further along through this baptismal stage, humans will soon transcend it. Our society has been in place for eons and only now does it show similar signs."

"So?"

"So, maybe it isn't the prospect of human interlopers that troubles them so much as the fear that there is a species that is progressing exponentially faster than them. And they know that some day, unless they act, they will be rendered obsolete and all their power will vanish."

"But isn't humanity inherently dangerous? Isn't it possible that long before they overtake the universe they could destroy themselves?"

"Bah! More garbage fed to you by the Council. Such blatant hypocrisy. Of course humans fight with one another for dominion. All species do in their early epochs. Even those plants who are so quick to preach about their utopian society. All empires are founded on conquest. Plants who stretched over others to choke out the light of rivals; strangled the roots of other plants with their own; cluttered entire planets with themselves, spreading to every nook and cranny. How is this any different from humanity? Yes, humanity is in great, great danger. But, unlike plants during their evolution, not just from themselves."

"So, how do we help them?" asked Hedge, then added an afterthought. "Should we help them?"

"Perhaps. They're the reason I'm here, you know. Isolated. Replaced by a didactic clod. I suggested we watch them. Because their potential was so great, but often their compassion appeared lacking. They learn so quickly, and at the same time so slowly. We have been around for so long, and yet they are gaining on us in a comparatively short amount of time. They are a marvel whose advancement accelerates and compassion swells, while we, I fear, do the opposite. It is perhaps because we are frightened by them. We become more like they were in an effort to be what they are not, giving us the option to point back at them and say 'They are different, and their difference is their undoing.'"

"They want me to lead the expedition to store them."

"Yes, I know," said the Plant. "It's perfect. The daisies are very clever. I've always thought daisies were the smartest of plants. Always thinking. It's because they grow so fast. They get accustomed to doing things at a faster pace. So much quicker in mind than those old trees, so slow to change, so rooted in the old ways. No pun intended." The Plant mumbled in distracted amusement.

"Perfect? They're doomed to eternal imprisonment."

"No no no. Not if *you* are the one abducting them."

"Oh! I hadn't thought of that."

Now he understood. As head of the project Hedge would be responsible for keeping track of all the humans that were stored and where they were kept. It would be very easy to misplace a few here and there.

"But how many should I take?" asked Hedge. "Five? Ten? And which ones? How do I choose who is most important?"

"Ah. You don't."

"I don't understand. You don't know how many?"

"How many? Ha! All of them!"

"All of them?"

"Yes. Not just the great and brilliant, but the fools and criminals as well. To segregate them now would create lopsided chaos. They must find their own equilibrium. Once you have them all, take them away to a new place where we have yet to expand. Refashion their world."

"Find an undiscovered planet, then refashion the whole world as it was? That could take millennia!"

"Certainly. Any job worth doing is worth the time. In exchange for this knowledge I have one demand."

Hedge braced himself.

"You must take me as well."

"But... you're the Plant of Ultimate Knowing. Someone is sure to notice. To come looking."

"Oh, I doubt that. I'm sure they'll be glad to be rid of me. Besides. This place is so dull."

The nearest acolyte moved, its long tentacles twisting, and lowered an appendage toward Hedge. Wrapped in the green tentacle was an orange, ceramic pot, which it set in the dirt beside the Weed of Ultimate Knowing. Hedge stared for a second, then realized what he was supposed to do.

"Thanks," he said.

The acolyte bent fractionally at the top in acknowledgment.

Despite its claims to the contrary, the Weed had proven its genius. It had expected this meeting but foreseen the outcome.

Hedge dug carefully around the weed with his hand, then down a few inches into the ground, and hauled up a ball of dirt with the weed and set it all in the pot. He took a few handfuls of the dark sod and tamped it into the gaps until it was firm but not hard. Plants found it terribly uncomfortable to have their roots packed into hard dirt, just as Hedge found it uncomfortable walking around in pants that were too tight.

It was warm and sleepy in the garden now, the pleasant afternoon light causing all it touched within the dome to fall into a drowsy swoon.

... hrm... never work... the giant sunflower mumbled in its sleep. find you... catch you...

"Shut up, you mindless drone!" called the weed, then turned its attention back to Hedge. "We'll have to be relatively quick. The Council controls this Plant, so it will know you are up to something and will likely send an agent to investigate."

A sense of foreboding fell over Hedge and he was assaulted by a flurry of thoughts. Take all of them? This would be a long task. How would he keep track of them? How would he know where they all went when he put them back? Where was he going to put them in the first place?

Hedge picked up the Weed of Ultimate Knowing and cradled it under one arm, the toaster under the other. This was quite an intimidating mission. He was nervous and worried. None of the acolytes seemed to pay him any attention. What if something went wrong and they were caught? What if he botched the abduction and all humanity was lost? What about Anna and Scud and all the others? Hedge was almost shaking with all the worry wound up inside him.

"Great!" said the Weed of Ultimate Knowing as they left the dome. Defiant and treasonous. They were a weed and a very frightened plant-man, armed with nothing but a toaster and a scarcely formulated plan assaulted on all sides by the possibility of calamity and disaster. "How exciting!"

ABDUCTION

On a worn yellow couch patterned with flowers a round woman in a nightgown sat staring at the television, arms wrapped around drawn-in knees. It was just after noon and her face was flushed and wet, the lower lip caught behind her teeth to keep it from shaking. Hair normally pulled into a tight bun hung down in random medusan straggles, her eyes were puffed and tired. All the curtains were drawn, but the day had not brightened beyond a muted gray and the air was heavy with gloom. Two days had passed since Hedge left to visit his brother in New Jersey. She had heard nothing since.

There was no brother in New Jersey. Anna knew that. Which could only mean one thing: another woman.

The news program prattled on as she drifted from one miserable thought to another.

... detected the objects four hours ago, hovering just beyond the upper atmosphere... President has yet to make a statement... Doctor Charles Rogerford, an astronomer and observer operating the powerful radio telescope in Puerto Rico for SETI, will attempt to shed some light on the nature of this phenomenon...

Doctor Rogerford was a middle-aged man with a silver-streaked beard and sharp eyes that exuded precision and intelligence. The eyes reminded her of Hedge, whom she often found staring at her as though he were taking her apart and putting her back together in his head. It was what intelligent people did. Figured out how things worked, why they worked, and so understood and appreciated them better. Rogerford stood outside a small building at the steel feet of a giant antenna, smiling with gentle enthusiasm. Below his head was an informational graphic which included his name, title and the acronym SETI, which expanded into Search for Extra-Terrestrial Intelligence.

This is a very exciting time for us, for all humanity, said Rogerford. *Throughout our existence...*

50

His voice trailed off as Anna's vision glazed.

It seemed as though something very important was happening, but she couldn't concentrate well enough to figure out what. If Hedge were here he would take the time to explain it to her very slowly even though he knew she wouldn't understand. It didn't matter. He enjoyed explaining and she loved listening. But the point was moot because Hedge was gone.

Why did men grow tired of the women who loved them so tirelessly? How did they forget what made them so beautiful, reducing them to just another rose in the flowerbed?

Anna's mind meandered in search of answers to her own questions. Because she was older now; because the pork chops were poor; because he needed something new and vibrant to hold his interest. This fear had always lurked at the rear of her mind, the fear that he would someday realize he was too good for her, but she had hoped and loved and quietly thanked, choosing to ignore the silent alarms in her head because there was nothing she could do to prevent him from going if he ever stopped loving her.

Hedge had always been distant, it was his nature, what made him so mysterious and alluring, and what made the bits of love he gave her so wonderful, so she never suspected he would leave until he was already gone. Without him there was no one. She had a vague recollection of family, of parents, but trying to remember brought feelings of discomfort and a strange burning in her mind as though something forbidden was coming unzipped.

Most days Anna felt energetic, rolling pleasantly from one chore to the next until the end of the day when she would lie beside Hedge and hold her book. She rarely read any of it, but it felt comfortable and familiar in her hands, and Hedge would sit next to her and stare. It was her favorite part of the day, when she had his whole attention, and all else was just a prelude.

She sighed.

Today she was just tired.

The newscaster became steadily more frantic as he related the newest reports. His tie was loose and the top of his shirt unbuttoned far enough to reveal the white undershirt beneath. A flurry of information scurried along the bottom of the screen in a thin bar while maps popped up, highlighted by dark red blotches like a spreading sunburn, followed by a reporter standing in an urban area while sirens wailed in the background.

... have just learned the President and his cabinet are unaccounted for in what appears to be a mass abduction. There have been no ransoms issued, and no countries or terrorist groups have claimed responsibil...

The picture flattened to a line and went silent in mid sentence, and Anna set the remote on the coffee table and lay back on the couch. Something dramatic was taking place, something global and extraordinary. It was possible this was the sort of world-changing event everyone would remember and later ask one another *Where were you when...?* Yet Anna found herself strangely indifferent. Maybe because she knew no matter what happened her answer would be *Alone*.

* * *

Hedge stared in silence at the giant, blue globe through the observation window at the bow of the craft, fascinated by the deceptive calm. Clouds wrapped slowly around it like soapy film while below, tiny and unseen, countless organisms doddered hither and thither across the surface, placid and unaware they were being watched.

In one hand he held a potted plant, though not so much a plant as a weed, which remained silent and dumb so no one would suspect its true nature.

Several other humanoid plants were on this ship, including John Elm, and the thousands of other ships encircling the planet, awaiting Hedge's word to start the process of extraction. To bring this entire civilization to an end. It was tragic to think humanity could never improve upon the works and accomplishments it had achieved thus far, and the thought filled Hedge with grief.

"Hedge?" asked John.

They had been here for several minutes, waiting for his order to commence. Not that other plants were unsettled by delay. Plants lived their entire lifespans without shifting positions, their existence gradually expended in idleness. But John was a motile plant such as Hedge, and waiting made him restless. There was no purpose in hesitation. Everything was in place, ready to begin. Everything but Hedge.

As Hedge watched the planet he raised a hand between it and himself, obscuring the whole thing, which seemed profound since he knew the planet was many hundreds of millions times larger than his hand. It was a simple matter of perspective. For some reason he suddenly remembered his trips with Anna to the small white building she called church, where she, Hedge, and perhaps forty other locals sat in an open room on very uncomfortable benches that made his back ache and his butt sore while one person stood at the far end of the chamber and pontificated in a loud and dramatic voice about the life of still another person whose father had created everything. Why so much attention was paid to the son of this great man, Hedge had no idea, as the one who created everything seemed far more noteworthy, and Anna frequently had to prevent Hedge from raising his hand and asking what she deemed *Impertinent Questions*. They called the father of this man, who wasn't really a man at all, but a creature of limitless power, God.

God reputedly knew everything, saw everything, was everywhere and was capable of everything within and without imagination because he had created everything and could thus shape it to his will—an elaborate human version of the Plant of Ultimate Knowing. Yet this God never displayed His powers in any conspicuous fashion as the great Plant had by advising the Council, and Hedge could not detect the presence of an omnipotent force watching over him and everything else. It was strange that he'd never heard of this God until he'd come to live amongst the humans. How was it they knew about Him and no one else did? Why did God choose to reveal Himself to these people? Why did so many refer to this God as a He, rather than She, It, or something else altogether, deigning to relate to this supreme being in their own terms? Like the Plant of Ultimate Knowing, everyone knew of God, but no one knew anything about him.

God was puzzling, elusive, exhausting, and scarcely believable.

Yet standing before the window looking down upon the planet where he knew none could see him, Hedge had a faint sense of familiarity with this God. For some reason being here, unseen, with plans for saving this race from what equated to annihilation, he understood how it might be possible for an entity with power over Hedge to be watching him from a similar position inside their own starship just outside the globe of the cosmos, obscuring the whole thing by passing a hand before his face, perhaps guiding Hedge away from disaster with deft and subtle alterations to his universe.

The thought boggled him as he gazed down at the planet.

Somewhere among the billions of these people, faintly aware or completely oblivious of the fate hanging over them, was a single human in a farmhouse. Hedge wondered what Anna was doing right now, wondered if she would notice when they came for her. Wondered if she even realized he'd left, or cared that he'd yet to return. Somewhere down there she busied herself with fewer chores, having just one person to trouble with, and perhaps found herself happier for it.

Hedge suffered a sudden rush of ridiculousness.

Maybe he could hurry to the planet and join her. The abduction would continue, but perhaps he could be taken with the humans and placed in storage as well. It didn't much matter to him that he would be in storage. Time would stop for him and all of humanity, and resume, if ever, when they were released. It wouldn't be so bad. He would be awake with Anna for a little while, and even should they never be revived, he would be in the place where he felt most comfortable, most useful, most... well, loved.

John Elm stood nearby, a constant, disconcerting presence. He watched Hedge with a look of perplexity and extreme curiosity, as if he were trying to figure out the puzzle of Hedge's facial expressions, trying to guess what Hedge was thinking and why these thoughts appeared to trouble him so. He would stare at Hedge, then stare at the weed Hedge had been toting around with him since returning from the garden of the Plant of Ultimate Knowing.

Was John an agent sent by the Council of Plants to watch Hedge? The more Hedge thought about it, the more likely it seemed.

John had asked him about visiting the Plant of Ultimate Knowing, why he had gone, and Hedge replied that he wanted to know how best to accomplish this task, which was more or less the truth.

John could not possibly guess the weed's significance. It simply wasn't remarkable enough to meet the expectations historical propaganda had created, but certainly John was bright enough to suspect something because no one else bothered carrying around a potted weed. He must suspect something, though he didn't know what, because John continued staring relentlessly with pinched and puzzled eyes.

Hedge turned to avoid his gaze.

A red blip on the console beside Hedge indicated the humans had detected them. There was no more time to delay.

Hedge let out a long breath of air and looked back to the plants awaiting his command.

"Okay," said Hedge. "Let's begin."

* * *

A knock at the door jerked Anna out of a half daze. She stood groggily and moved through the kitchen, brushing past the table where smears of grease remained from the broken toaster, wondering Why should I bother? She asked herself this same question twice more before she reached the door, at which point she decided it would be rude not to answer.

When she opened the door a tall, pale man stood in the opening. He was dressed in black and wore sunglasses so dark she couldn't see the outline of his eyes behind them. He wore an extremely large, but crooked smile, as though he were both very excited and very uncertain about being on the porch. His hands were at his waist and in them was a toaster.

"You have one, too," Anna remarked.

The visitor seemed momentarily alarmed, as though she'd discovered a secret he'd meant to keep to himself.

"It's just a toaster," he said.

"Yes," said Anna. "I know. Can I help you?"

"I think so," said the visitor.

He appeared distracted, looking over his shoulder toward one side of the porch then the other as if he expected someone to arrive.

"Who are you?" asked Anna.

"My name is Mr. Visitor," said Mr. Visitor. He seemed very pleased by his name. "I'm looking for Mr. Hedge."

Anna scowled.

"He's in New Jersey," she said, and closed the door.

Anna could see Mr. Visitor's silhouette through the drapes over the door's window, and she waited for him to leave so she could skulk back to the couch, but he remained motionless for some time. In fact, it was a while before he made any movement at all. A minute passed before she saw his shoulders sink, then he turned away from the door, took a few steps, and vanished.

For an instant her curiosity flared and she thought about opening the door to confirm he was still there and hadn't disappeared in a puff of smoke. But she was overcome by a strong feeling of lethargy and a feeling that it didn't really matter, so she returned to the couch and lay down.

At the same time, the world around, people began to disappear.

* * *

At first no one seemed to notice. One person would not show up to a job interview or a dentist appointment. Then another would leave for the lavatory or for lunch or to investigate a noise in another room and not come back. A few scattered incidents, like the opening scenes in a horror film but without the mutilated bodies and psychopathic murderers. It wasn't until people of prominence began to go missing that anyone really took notice.

News programs began spreading reports of disappearing officials, then ended abruptly when the reporters went missing. Law enforcement agents commenced investigations only to vanish themselves.

There were a lot of them. Several billion to be more precise. They were frantic when at last they realized something mysterious and methodical and strange was going on, but those who could do something or spread information were taken amongst the first, so news traveled slowly, and ultimately there was nothing to be done. Well planned, well executed.

All told, the extraction took slightly over six hours. The condensing of human civilization, gathering the abducted from all the ships into a single container, a thin glass beaker, took two minutes. The trip back to planet Plant took as long as it would have taken to toast a single slice of bread.

They were asleep now. Preserved, compacted, all of the mechanisms required to keep them living and unconscious were tiny enough to fit within the confines of a small vial. Along with the lot of humanity. And the vial was small enough to fit within an inside jacket pocket. And Hedge, formidable and round, was just small enough to fit within such a jacket.

As the designated Commander of the Abduction of Humanity fleet, it was Hedge's responsibility to take their condensed species to the Records Vault for indefinite storage. There they would remain, alongside samples of dinosaur and dodo, sperm whale and brine shrimp, and countless other species from their world and others, until humanity was deemed ready to be reintroduced into the social fabric of the universe or if the plants found some use for them. To date, no species placed in storage had ever been revived.

Hedge made his way through the chest-high hedges on his way to the great spire where the records of countless other species were kept. He passed other plants in silence, each with their own urgent errands. It was sunny today, and breezy enough to blow away the mugginess. Bright and pleasant as some of the nicest days Hedge had spent with humanity. It seemed as though he would complete this mission without the slightest interruption. This was, to Hedge, a great relief.

"Hello, Hedge."

The voice was familiar, and when Hedge looked to the side there was John Elm, tall and imposing, striding alongside him.

"Hello, John."

Hedge tried to walk faster, worried John would begin asking him about what he was thinking and planning, but doing so with such a round body made him tired and John had no trouble keeping pace.

"Where is your weed, Hedge?" he asked.

"What weed?"

John was undeterred.

"The weed you've been carrying around with you. The one you brought back from the garden. The one you took on the ship. The one you were whispering to during the abduction. That weed."

"Oh," said Hedge. John had been watching more closely than Hedge suspected. "I don't have it any more. I took it back. It was just a weed."

They were fast approaching the empty swath around the spire and Hedge puffed with the effort as he tried to keep up a rapid pace. He could not outrun John, but he could shorten the encounter if he could get to the vault before John asked too many difficult questions.

"I see," said John. "I guess you're going to the records vault, then. You have the vial with you right now?"

"Yes," Hedge puffed. "To both."

John made a few gurgling noises in his throat as though two phrases were fighting for dominance and only the victor would emerge.

"Can I see it?" he asked at last.

"I'm afraid not," said Hedge quickly. "I can't afford to let anything happen."

"Yes, oh, yes," said John. He stopped. "I understand. Well, here we are. I suppose this is where we part ways."

"Yes, John," said Hedge, trying hard not to gasp. "I'm sorry we couldn't continue our discussion. Perhaps another time."

"Another time," John repeated.

Hedge turned away, face burning.

He approached the towering spire of the records vault, feeling John's eyes upon him until he passed into the wide chamber and strode to the solitary pneumatic tube that would whisk the vial a storage location.

He stood inside the building, out of view of John, his breath rasping, then continued on when he recovered.

A vaguely human plant sat in the center of several thousand labeled buttons. For as much as humans were despised, it was generally acknowledged that their basic arrangement of appendages was oftentimes quite handy.

The plant looked at him with a single eye situated at the intersection of its many limbs. Its empty gaze bespoke long exposure to a deep and numbing boredom so that it was scarcely aware of anything at all. There was no joy or sadness, it lacked all concept of such feelings. Existence was no more than just that, the plant simply Was and nothing else. Purely functional, like a snow shovel or a shoelace. Hedge felt a great swell of pity for the plant.

"Withdrawal," it asked in a slow, robotic tone. More statement than question.

Hedge shook his head in negation.

"Deposit."

The plant accepted this answer in silence. Withdrawals never happened.

There was no banter. No flimsy words to fill the silence. The other plant simply logged the information dispassionately, then continued the pre-programmed inquiry.

"Genus species."

"*Homo sapiens sapiens*," Hedge answered.

"Photoautotroph?"

"Omnivore."

"Terrestrial?"

"Yes."

"Quadrapedal?"

"Bipedal."

The plant tugged on a few pulleys, pressed a button here and there, then handed him a label and a cushioned, cylindrical vessel.

"Place the vial in the vessel. Place the label on the vessel. Place the vessel in the tube."

Hedge took the vial from his pocket, pressed it into the vessel, pressed the label onto the vessel with his thumb, and set the vessel in the pneumatic tube in the center of the room. There was a momentary hesitation, then a sucking whoosh, and the vial was gone, spinning somewhere overhead through the spiderweb of connecting tubework on its course to permanent storage. He tried to watch it as long as he could, but could only track the vessel through the first two turns before he lost sight of it.

"Thank you," said the plant in disinterested monotone.

Rather than answer, Hedge simply turned and left. When he emerged, John Elm was nowhere to be seen.

Hedge meandered for a while through the hedges and shrubbery, aimlessly wandering. He looked about every once in a while, afraid he would see John Elm poke his head around the corner or find him peering over the bushes, watching. At last he stopped beside an outcropping of ferns with wide umbrella canopies hovering just above the ground and sat. Heaved a long breath.

"Okay," he said. "Now what?"

Situated just behind the first layer of foliage was a small, potted weed with two red leaves at its top. The stoppered mouth of a small vial protruded from the dark dirt beside the stem.

"Now," said the Plant of Ultimate Knowing, "we figure out where to put them."

A BRIEF VISIT

I am an excellent guard, thought Trunk the guard. I am very excellent, he reasoned, because no one ever goes through the council entrance without first being announced.

Trunk stood outside the entrance to the Council of Plants. He was the only guard outside the council entrance because, he assumed, he was very good at what he did. What made one good at Trunk's job, he decided, was to be very large, because that is what he was. Trunk had a stocky shape with thick brown bark and two long branches he would use to hold out in front of anyone who tried to enter the council without being announced. Nothing of the sort ever happened, but he imagined it would go something like that if it ever did.

Trunk must have nodded off, because abruptly there was a being standing in front of him. The creature had the look of several plant agents who recently returned to provide testimony that some far-off planet needed to be destroyed. Hyoo-munns or some such. Like those agents, he too carried a toaster. All his features appeared symmetrical except his mouth, which was slightly askew and maybe too large.

The character's appearance was so peculiar Trunk realized with embarrassment that he'd forgotten his duty.

"Who are you?" asked Trunk. "Why are you here?"

"I am Mr. Visitor." Mr. Visitor pointed to his feet. "I am here due to a slight miscalculation. I meant to be there."

Mr. Visitor stared at the doors leading into the chamber.

"Have you been announced?" asked Trunk. When Mr. Visitor did not respond immediately, Trunk continued. "You cannot enter without being announced. It would be very bad if you entered before being announced."

The two stood in silence for a moment, awaiting an announcement.

"How bad?" Mr. Visitor asked at last.

Trunk wanted very much to have a strong and compelling answer to this question, but since it had never happened before, he didn't.

"I don't know."

"I see," said Mr. Visitor. He looked down at his toaster and turned his thumb against the side. After a moment he pressed a lever on the side of the toaster and looked back up at Trunk. "My apologies for any inconvenience this may cause you."

Mr. Visitor took a step forward.

At this point Trunk's training took over and he slid his massive body between Mr. Visitor and the door. He held out a great, gnarled hand, against which he expected the visitor would run into, and, finding no way around him, admit defeat and wait until he'd been announced.

To Trunk's surprise, there was nothing to strike his open hand but a warm wave of air. The visitor had gone. Trunk looked behind him, yet found nothing but the doors, still shut. The two footprints in the dirt remained, but no tracks led to, nor away from them. He waved a hand through the air above the footprints, suspecting the fellow might somehow have turned himself invisible, but only stirred up a faint odor of something burning that went away quickly.

"Hum," said Trunk, perplexed.

He considered wandering from his post to search for Mr. Visitor, then considered the possibility that wandering from his post was exactly the result Mr. Visitor wanted. Trunk was too smart to be lured away, however, and he felt pleased that he had not been so gullible.

This sense of pleasure gave way to curiosity as a sound of uproar grew behind the doors. Knowing this was against protocol, but feeling clever and heroic at the moment, Trunk threw open the doors and lunged inside, confident he could resolve any issue.

A great deal of shouting was going on from the plants arranged throughout the council, full of bile and outrage, all of which seemed to be focused on a single point at the base of the room. At the epicenter Trunk found Mr. Visitor, looking back at him with his great crooked grin on his face.

Trunk's mind boggled.

"Hello," said Mr. Visitor pleasantly, as if his presence here was completely within the boundaries of protocol.

Trunk stood motionless, too flabbergasted to reply. As he stood, the incoherent howling of the council thundering down upon him became understandable when he began to pick out small chunks.

"Stop him!" they cried. "Catch him!"

"What are you doing in here?" Trunk asked at last.

"Warning them," said Mr. Visitor. "That's what I do. It never works, though. Are you familiar with a Mr. Hedge?"

Trunk thought.

"No."

Mr. Visitor seemed disappointed but unsurprised.

"He is a very elusive character," he confessed.

"I have to catch you," said Trunk. "It's my job."

"I understand," said Mr. Visitor.

Mr. Visitor was extremely polite, Trunk decided, despite the fact that the council seemed to think he meant to destroy them. It didn't seem the case to Trunk, though. He expected a destroyer, such as the Fire-tailed Xiz, would appear more menacing. As a result, Trunk was only mildly disappointed when Mr. Visitor vanished when Trunk clapped his arms around the intruder, leaving behind another set of empty footprints and a smell of burning.

The clamor grew louder at Mr. Visitor's disappearance, but Trunk knew he couldn't do any more. So he left the council, closed the doors behind him, and resumed his duties. It didn't make sense to get all worked up when they could always just ask the Plant of Ultimate Knowing what to do.

A NEW GARDEN

Hedge stared dully at the display as stars and systems and galaxies buzzed past, orange and blue nebula bursts of exploded suns still expanding after millions of years. His back and arms and butt were sore from sitting at the terminal, where it seemed he'd spent the past several days. It made him wonder how trees remained locked in a single position for their entire lifespan, sometimes hundreds of years, without becoming crabby and plagued by countless, lingering aches. The Plant of Ultimate Knowing was on the desk at his elbow, maybe watching, maybe asleep. Hedge couldn't tell.

It was quiet and dark in this gothic and grim complex where all of the data plant society had gathered was kept and made available to any who wished to peruse it.

Right now Hedge was browsing three-dimensional displays of star charts, searching. As the Plant of Ultimate Knowing had explained, stealing humanity was simple. Saving them would prove most difficult, and would require a great deal of legwork. Stealing humanity wasn't enough to save them. Now they needed to find a place to hide them. But despite the tremendous area that plants governed and explored there were very few systems capable of supporting more than the simplest forms of life, and of the few that could support them there were none that weren't already occupied or being watched.

Now, as he stared blankly at the star systems that flickered on the screen, Hedge understood why the plants governing the universe had time for little else. Universe had always been understood as a vast, all-encompassing term, but he'd never quite grasped the sheer enormity until he tried to rifle through the whole thing without knowing where to look, and thus having to look everywhere. There was just so much. Little wonder the plants where humans lived never bothered to evolve and left the rule of the planet to others. There was no time for relaxation, no time for joy. Maybe these plants were wisest, rather than those who sat in the Council chamber. And Hedge realized yet again why it was he so enjoyed his time with Anna. There were no disasters of galactic proportion to fret about, and never more than the slightest interruptio....

"There!"

The Plant of Ultimate Knowing's quiet but biting voice jerked him from his reverie.

Hedge blinked rapidly and his surroundings retook focus.

The scene had fixed on a small star system with a single solar body and several planets of varying sizes. Some ringed with moons, others surrounded by rings of debris which might have been moons. They orbited a rather small, middle-aged star, which grew larger as the weed manipulated the view through means Hedge could not detect. When it stopped moving forward there was a planet in the center of the display, the third in the system and one of the smaller of them.

"That's it!" said the Plant.

"It's kind of small," Hedge observed.

"It's perfect."

Hedge shrugged and leaned in for a closer look. There were bands of white running across the blue planet, just as there had been on the old world, and continents were crusty plates of brown and green. Maybe there were animals there already, thought Hedge. Maybe some other sentient creature, perhaps, that could teach humanity to behave themselves. Maybe, with time, the Council of plants would forget their initial decision and allow humanity to join their administration. Or maybe humans would prove to be the doom of the universe after all and ruin it for everyone.

As he leaned closer, to see if he could detect any signs of civilization, the whole display went suddenly white, then shut off.

"What happened!?" cried Hedge.

Had the star gone suddenly nova as they were watching? The odds of such a coincidence were staggering. It was amazing and tragic. But the star was so small, and relatively young as well. It was neither old enough nor large enough to explode. Unless someone had blown it up.

"I erased it," said the Plant. "No one else should know. That should give us a head start."

Hedge let out a puff of air. That made sense. If there was no record of the system, the other plants couldn't very well go looking for humans there. Then again, if there were no record of the system, there was also no way of knowing where it was located.

"But how will *we* find it?"

"I can find it," the Plant assured him.

"What about when they discover this area of unexplored space? Won't they come to investigate to complete their records? What will we do then?"

"That's assuming anyone bothers to check. For all they know, it's just a very tiny, mostly vacant smudge of universe, just like the majority of the rest. The likelihood of being discovered and caught is very, very slim at best. The Universe, as I'm sure you know by now, is a very big place."

Hedge decided the weed must be correct and, feeling greatly relieved, stood up, tucked the pot under his arm and began to move away from the terminal. What could possibly happen? The answer, as the weed had made patently clear, was nothing.

"Stop!"

The voice was tiny with distance but grew larger when it repeated. Coming closer.

Hedge stiffened. If he bolted it would only draw more attention. So close! How did they know? Had John Elm figured out what he was up to and alerted the Council? If so he'd surely be mulched. A wave of sadness swept over him. Not just for himself, but for the Plant of Ultimate Knowing and humanity as well. Soon he would be surrounded by troopers who would take him to a makeshift Mulchitorium and that would be the end of him, the end of the Plant of Ultimate Knowing and the end of humanity. Thrice a failure.

But no. He couldn't allow this to happen. Not to Anna. Not to everyone and everything. Maybe he could bluff his way out of this. Plants weren't accustomed to deception so they might be fooled by it. As he had learned from humanity, the best way for the guilty to elude prosecution was to behave as though they had done nothing wrong.

When he turned, John Elm was running toward him and several more lingered in his steps. John huffed and gasped for a few moments after he arrived, folded at the waist, and looked up occasionally as though he were about to speak, then receded back into gasping. Hedge's mind raced for an appropriate lie in the meantime.

Why was he in possession of the humanity he was supposed to file away? There must be a mistake. No no. That wouldn't work. I'm going to visit my brother in New Jersey. No. That hadn't even worked on Anna. Anna. How he missed her. The awful pork chops, her persistent questions, her fascination with the misery of her fellow humans, the way she wanted nothing more than to want him to want her.

"I know what you're doing," John Elm said at last.

Curses! His mind had drifted and the advantage was lost. What to do? He recalled reading about humans captured by the legal system who became frantic when faced with the reality of their crime, their mind darting wildly and swelling with the prospect of repudiation, and ultimately confessed all to relieve the burden of their guilt. They were punished all the same. Yet all those who avoided punishment seemed to share similar characteristics in that they were more collected, kept a clear head, and utilized the lone, unfailing tactic which remained available to them: Deny Everything.

"No you don't," Hedge replied.

John seemed momentarily confused, then he continued.

"I know what you're doing," he repeated. "You're hiding them from the others. So they can't destroy humanity. And I wanted to know..."

His eyes drifted here and there as though suspicious someone might be listening. So it was a bribe! A very human sort of corruption. He would have to buy the silence of John Elm. But how? What could Hedge possess which John couldn't get from anyone else? John's voice grew quieter.

"I wanted to know if we could go, too."

Hedge was too surprised to respond.

"We have to leave now," John continued. "We're being followed."

"How did the Council find out?" asked the Plant.

"They don't know. Not yet. It isn't the Council. It's a Visitor. The Council is tearing the planet apart looking for it. And you. It knows you, Hedge. It asked for you by name."

Hedge remained speechless.

"Well then," said the Plant. "We had best be on our way."

AWAKENING

Hedge tapped a nail into the skeleton of a half-completed fence, just deep enough to hold it in place. Then he lined up the shaft and smashed the nail into the wood up to the hilt. The single strike echoed across the cornfield.

The first fence he'd tried to build, before the abduction, was filled with crooked, jutting nails. The uneven rails and red, swollen fingers were a testament to his poor carpentry skills. Hedge flexed his fingers, recalling the wooden smell from the hammer blows and the keen, stabbing throb in the tips of his hands. He'd never felt pain until the fat metal hammerhead came down on his fingernail, and his anguish was so blinding that it was some time before he could accept the pain for what it was: instructive. There was a lesson in pain, and the effects were immediate.

This time was for making things better.

At that moment he understood, far better than he had before when he studied their histories and their political structures before he arrived, what it was to be human. Their whole existence was centered upon suffering. That was the first time he considered humanity's massive potential. They made frequent mistakes, yes, but if those mistakes were adequately painful they made every effort to avoid repeating them, to improve upon their errors. To be more careful so they didn't catch their thumb under the hammerhead.

It made sense why their history was alternately tragic and astounding. With each disaster came new awareness. The only worry was that one day the disaster might be so traumatic and devastating there would be no recovery. This was probably the initial concern of the Council of Plants.

Of course, the Council of Plants believed that dilemma had been mitigated.

Hedge grinned.

On the other hand, humanity might one day be able to judge the results of their actions before they took them. In essence, to see the hammer blow before it fell. That is what he, and the others who joined him, were hoping.

Rows of corn bent at the peak like the bristles of an overused broom; the willow commanded the open area beside the thin, dirty road that vanished into the forest; the blue sky faded from orange to purple as the sun departed.

Hedge and the others were happy to discover the new planet was just as lovely as the last. Many of the species which populated the previous world existed in similar form here, too. Dogs and cats and lions and ostriches and penguins, though they still had to make several covert trips back to the original planet to procure those plants and animals the humans called pets but kept as friends.

Hedge toiled endlessly, reviewing the stories of their lives, trying to refashion the world as they remembered it, but with a touch of change here and there based on suggestions by the plants who accompanied him. A few extra plants, more poignant histories from which to learn, more pleasant thoughts from the past. John Elm, who had been a grocer, recommended more bananas.

Bananas, John explained, contain tryptophan, which the human body converts to relaxing seratonin; contain potassium, which lowers blood pressure and raises alertness, which facilitates learning and thought; is high in fiber and restores normal bowel action; is a natural antacid; soothes intestinal disorders; lowers the chance of stroke. Even the inside of the banana skin was useful in reducing the swelling and irritation of mosquito bites.

Most times he found himself thinking of Anna, reviewing her story in particular, the countless times she would be watching him without his knowing, how she spent every moment of their existence trying to please him and feeling as though she was in danger of failing, the days she spent after he left before the abduction. It was the sight of those moments which he agonized over most because he had hurt her, unwittingly, and she felt as though he'd forsaken her. He agonized over the thought that he'd betrayed her confidence and broken something that could never be mended.

Days and months and weeks and years and more blended together into an indistinguishable morass, and Hedge sometimes found himself trying to remember why they had started this project. Was it just so he could see Anna again, or was there a greater purpose? It troubled him to think everything he had done was humanly selfish, that there was no other reason for saving humanity than to save one person. And to save that person for himself. That, he noted, seemed keenly similar to the love she had expressed for him.

Hedge leaned back from the fence and sat.

It was during this moment, a few nails in his mouth and hammer in hand, his exhausted mind spinning thoughtlessly, when a figure approached and stood before him. The figure stopped between Hedge and the setting sun, and a shining corona silhouetted the person with a golden blaze as if the visitor were some biblical entity sent to place him on the path to righteousness, or punish him violently for straying.

Human religions were filled with stories of divine intervention, with angels and demons and gods and such visiting people to tell them what steps to take next because people believed themselves to be ignorant and didn't trust themselves to know where to go on their own. It filled Hedge with sudden hope to know a creature who supposedly knew everything, knew exactly what must be done, was here to aid him. It reassured him, as the myth of the Plant of Ultimate Knowing had granted a sense of righteousness to all he did before he learned the truth.

The figure crouched, the dazzle of light vanished, and the familiar features of John Elm came into focus. He looked tired, or gray, or somehow different than Hedge recalled. How long had they been doing this?

John looked at the incomplete fence, then looked back at Hedge.

"What are you doing?" he asked. His voice was older and raspy, like soft-splintered wood.

"Thinking," Hedge replied, though he was unsure he'd been doing anything of the sort. "I think."

John extended a hand toward Hedge.

"Banana?" he asked.

"No, thanks."

John shrugged, peeled the banana, and began to eat it.

"Thinking about what?"

"I think... wondering why we were doing this," Hedge decided. "Maybe whether we should. What will it accomplish? Was the Council right? What if humanity is a dangerous failure? What if I'm doing this for myself and the result is disaster?"

John stood again. Set one hand on his hip and took a deep breath. His features became shrouded and the light gave him a supernatural glow. All that prevented the figure from appearing divine was the propeller shape of a peeled banana still in his hand.

"Wonder the same thing every now and again," said John. "Helps to think of horoscopes."

"Horoscopes?"

Horoscopes, as Hedge recalled, were another trivial tidbit which delighted Anna. Presumably, they foretold the future for groups of people born during a certain time of year. When Hedge investigated, he found the horoscopes were vague, perhaps purposefully, simple statements that could be made to apply to anyone. Sometimes their predictions were horribly incorrect, but that did not dissuade her from taking pleasure in the rare paragraph that was right.

"Horoscopes and fortune cookies and little candy hearts with loving phrases," John continued. "Reminds me they search everywhere for glimmers of hope to inspire them."

Hedge recalled Anna telling him that on the night they met she'd read a horoscope that prophesied she would meet someone from far away who would bring her lasting happiness. It had come true, she said, so it was entirely possible another could be equally right.

Of course, Hedge knew that was not the case. The idea of that particular horoscope had either been an invention of those who rewrote her history or an invention of her own mind. It took very little convincing to make humans believe what they wanted to believe.

"But they are all false," said Hedge. "There is no true clairvoyance."

"Trueness or falseness isn't the point. It's the search that's important. Makes me remember my earthchildren and their initial attempts to ride the two-wheeled vehicles... Manually propelled devices." John thumped a finger on his temple. "What are they called?"

"Bicycles."

"That's it. Bound and determined to ride those bicycles and always meeting with failure. Bruising themselves. Cursing themselves. But they persevered. Then, at the limit of their frustration, they asked me if they would ever be able to ride with the same ease as others. After some thought I answered them: Yes. I believed they could do it. It seemed a logical conclusion. All they required was repetition to familiarize themselves with the contraption and maintain their balance. Soon after, they did. At the same time I realized it wasn't so much the practice they needed, but faith. In fact, faith might have been all they required. That was my cathartic moment—when I realized humans have difficulty believing in themselves, but if someone believes in them, they can accomplish anything. They have reason to hope. It's why they look so often to their benevolent entities. They believe in those mighty beings in the hope that those mighty beings might believe in them. Deities exist for people, you see, not the other way around."

"What are you saying?"

"I'm saying that is why I decided to do this. Because I enjoy this place, but also because I think they can be great. Because I believe they can succeed. They can do truly amazing things, and I want to be witness to them. Consider my earthchildren and their bicycle. They want to succeed. Imagine the extraordinary effects of simply telling them they can."

* * *

Hedge stood on the lowest step of the staircase, arms stretched to their limit overhead, adjusting a picture frame until it was not quite level with the bookshelf beside it and the ship in the photo appeared to be sailing down a sloped ocean to the edge of the world. When he released it the picture righted itself.

Humans had once believed their world was no more than a shingle of land and water drifting through the ether, with no explanation for what happened if someone were to venture beyond the boundary. It was an ignorant perception of the past at which most scoffed, but those who were wiser simply shook their heads in embarrassment knowing similar fears and ignorance confronted them in different forms now. They would persist and overcome, just as they had before. In spite of a multitude of dissenters guided by a supernatural fear of the unknown, their logic would prevail in the end, and that was their salvation.

Or so he hoped.

Hedge stepped back, set his hands on his hips. Looked to a rusty wheelbarrow at his side where the Plant of Ultimate Knowing was seated. His eyes were somewhat filmy, the faint green of his skin was turning gray.

At the same time there was a crunch of gravel as John Elm walked up the stone driveway, clonked up the wooden porch stairs and pulled the door open. John's once hickory hair and eyebrows were ash colored. He nodded.

"That's it," he said.

Both of them looked at the wheelbarrow.

"Okay," said the Plant. "Let's wake them up."

Hedge turned to a table where a sheet rose over a small lump in the center. He yanked the sheet away and dust swirled above a coffee maker. In so many ways humanity was agonizingly close to one breakthrough or another, but they always seemed to be pointing the right machine in the wrong direction. The machine appeared no different from any other coffee maker with exception to two additional buttons John had marked with black marker on surgical tape: Awaken and Asleepen. Hedge flipped a toggle switch to On and the machine began to hum.

"Water," said Hedge, eyeing the machine. "So it doesn't overheat."

John left for the kitchen and returned with a bowl of water that he poured into the top of the coffee maker. The machine gurgled and began to drip.

"Before we do this, might we consider the consequences?"

Hedge look at John in puzzlement.

"What consequences?" asked Hedge.

John looked back, equally mystified.

"I didn't say anything," he responded.

Hedge looked at the Plant of Ultimate Knowing.

"Me either," it said.

"I said it."

Hedge and John turned.

A man stood before the doorway, though it remained closed behind him and there was no indication he'd used it to enter. A tremendous smile curled up one side of his face. He pressed a slipping pair of impenetrably black sunglasses against his face with a finger, then lowered the hand to his waist where he supported a silver toaster. That would explain how he got inside.

Hedge did not recognize him. Could humanity have awoken already? He checked the machine, but the Awaken button remained dark. They were still in stasis. The only explanation left was that plants had found them. No doubt they would not be lenient this time. Now it would be extermination. Hedge's shoulders slouched.

"Who are you?" asked John.

"I am not a plant, as you might suspect."

"Oh," said Hedge relieved.

"I am Mr. Visitor," the man said, "and I have been looking for you for a very, very long time."

"Oh," Hedge repeated, this time very much alarmed.

"A Visitor," murmured the Plant.

"Correct," said Mr. Visitor. His gaze wandered across the interior of the house. "It has been some time since I last visited. It is just as I remember. Remarkable." He squinted, inspecting the photo beside the bookcase. "Except that picture had more of a cant to it."

"An idiosyncrasy we were unable to duplicate," said the Plant.

"No. It is an improvement," Mr. Visitor remarked.

"You were here?" Hedge interrupted, astounded. "In this house?"

"Not *this* house, per se," said Mr. Visitor. "But… this house. Looking for you."

"And wherever you go, destruction follows," John added darkly.

Mr. Visitor tapped a finger against the toaster.

"That is the pattern. Thus far I have remained a step behind you."

"No longer, it would seem," said the Plant. "Why are you here? What have we done to earn destruction?"

Mr. Visitor cocked his head to one side.

"You? Nothing, I imagine. Individuals are not my concern. I am more interested in civilizations."

Hedge's sadness slowly gave way to uneasiness. The two of them seemed to be talking about the same thing, and though they appeared to understand what the other was talking about, both felt uncertain, as if the two ideas were grasping at one another's hands but hadn't yet taken hold.

"You destroy every civilization you encounter," Hedge explained.

Mr. Visitor blinked.

"Every civilization I encounter has met its end soon after. This is true. Correlation does imply causation." Mr. Visitor's eyes widened, understanding. "You believe my coming is a harbinger of doom. It is, in a way. I would otherwise have no reason for being here."

"I don't understand," said Hedge. "You are not here to destroy humanity, but humanity will be destroyed."

"Every civilization I encounter is either incapable of responding to the impending threat or refuses to admit its faults and amend them. None heed the warning. Not even my own people. They are, in all cases, the purveyors of their own destruction. My influence is painfully negligible."

"Your people…," the Plant of Ultimate Knowing echoed.

Mr. Visitor nodded.

"I am the last. For many millennia now."

"All the stories we tell," said John, "of so many encounters with Visitors. They are you. Always you. *Only* you."

Mr. Visitor nodded.

"Few species survive long enough to reach the point of civilization. Those few are fortunate to exist in a period where the many hazards of the universe do not befall during their development. It truly is a tragedy when a civilization survives so long, escaping so many perils, only to die by its own hand."

"Then who did you come to warn?" asked Hedge.

"I had meant to warn you that humanity stood upon such a precipice. I have found leaders of worlds have too much invested in their status to change anything. Instead, I sought someone who might value the people itself. Someone who would seek to save them. I am glad to say I was successful in locating such as person, though a bit late. Now my mission becomes asking you to consider the consequences of waking them. Consider waking them places them back upon their precipice."

Hedge raised a hand and flexed a somewhat flattened thumb, recalling his experiences building the fence.

"I know them well enough to know they can learn from their mistakes."

Mr. Visitor considered this. He did not seem to understand what this meant, though he did understand that Hedge would not be deterred.

"Very well. I have only one request. That Mr. Hedge join me in my travels."

Hedge frowned.

"I can't go."

"Why not? Your mission is complete. Almost."

"I think because I am *too* human," said Hedge. "As a human I pine for things just beyond reach and cleave to them when they wander near enough."

"I see," said Mr. Visitor. "They are very near now."

Hedge glanced at the coffee machine.

"Very," he agreed.

"You should stay," the Plant suggested. "You should join us rather than the other way round. See how this works out. It would do you good to see a success now and again."

Mr. Visitor hesitated.

"Perhaps," he said. "But where would I fit into your elaborate design?"

* * *

Considering the sheer volume of details to be reproduced, errors were inevitable. People who were certain they put watches on their right wrist were at a momentary loss until they found them on the left. Leaders of nations felt certain they had been little more than grocery store clerks the day before, while grocery store clerks were possessed by a strong impression that they had ruled nations not long ago. Despite some initial discomfort, these people found their new responsibilities and wristwatch locations more convenient and much to their liking. Former clerks fit snugly in their new positions; former presidents wondered how they had ever been capable of more than bagging groceries. Soon, all of them decided things could not have been any other way, and should those lingering dreams come true everyone would be the worse for it.

For the most part, nothing was changed. Across the world people were waking up, finding themselves right where they remembered, doing the things they knew best. Mail carriers delivering, politicians arguing, athletes competing, mathematicians adding. In a small midwest town a short man in a wrinkled shirt named Scud Peabody was greeted at Milo's Corner Diner with utmost respect, treated to free coffee by patrons who hung anxiously upon his every stammering word, fascinated by his sincerity, his clarity of thought, and a mind which moved with such rapidity that his sputtering mouth simply could not keep up.

Foremost among them was a man named Garry Thorne, who repeated Scud's words to other folk as though it were writ passed down from the burning summit of some holy mountain. It only made sense to be polite to Scud, as he could remember nothing but politeness throughout their relationship, and it filled him with a powerful joy that he wanted to spread everywhere: throughout the diner, throughout the town, to the places across the country where his delivery truck took him, even his own family which he loved and loved him in return. He knew full well, because Scud had said as much, that to love others was to be loved in return, and nothing brought him greater joy.

At the foot of a rosewood bed covered by a flowered comforter inside a two-story farmhouse surrounded by corn and honeybee hives was a wooden chair, and in that chair was a plant alien named Hedge. He watched. Waited. Just as he had before, for twenty years, though this time there would be no instructions. Life was his own and this was how he chose to spend it.

In the bed lay Anna, who had returned to consciousness as had everyone else, but had yet to rise from her slumber.

Her face was soft and round, and Hedge wanted very much to touch it but was afraid doing so would ruin the image, as if it were a reflection in a puddle. Humanity was lovely and serene in those untroubled moments between dreams. Her breath raised and lowered the sheets with a regular pulse and her eyebrows lifted as her mind ran through the labyrinth of interconnected fantasies. Hedge was enthralled by her symmetry, yet the word was too cool and dry. She was beautiful.

In the sill of the broad bedroom window full of light sat a thin weed, somewhat taller than when Hedge first encountered it. Two red leaves grew from the top, and a third hung from the tip of another branch extending from the middle of the stem.

Mr. Visitor sat on the sill beside the Plant, looking up into the sky.

It was possible plants might find them eventually. Maybe the Council would discover they'd been duped, but there was no indication so far. If they did, perhaps by then humanity would be better able to negotiate for themselves. Perhaps plants would be more ready to welcome them.

"What will my name be?" asked Mr. Visitor. "I gather Mr. Visitor was not as subtle as I hoped."

"Edwin," said Hedge. "You're my brother. From New Jersey."

"Very good," said the Plant.

"It is entirely possible they could revert to their miserable ways," said Mr. Visitor. "Perhaps they are innately cruel and barbarous with a few accidental flashes of inspiration and... well... humanity. It's possible we have imperiled the entire universe in the hope that they will come to their senses before it's too late. It's possible that doing as your Council asked was best."

"Maybe," said the Plant.

"Then what? What if they turn suddenly foul?"

"Then we do it again."

"That's not a solution."

"It isn't," the Plant agreed. "It's an opportunity. They need only take it."

"Hm. God help them," Mr. Visitor remarked. "If you believe in that metaphysical mumbo jumbo."

Hedge nodded.

"He has."

The Plant sounded amused.

"Yes. I suppose He has, hasn't He?"

The warm light streaming through the window made Hedge drowsy and he was drifting gradually toward slumber when a twitch beneath the covers brought him swiftly back to alertness.

At last, waking from a long and fitful sleep, Anna opened her bleary eyes, saw Hedge smiling at her and smiled in return. Maybe his skin seemed a bit baggier than she remembered, eyes a bit deeper, back a bit more stooped. Whatever was amiss she still loved him. Hedge could see it in her smile.

"I thought you were going to New Jersey," she said. "To see your brother."

Hedge shrugged, grinned wryly.

"I..." His mind raced with all the things he'd thought to tell her. Everything he realized he should have said before but was, like all people before their flash of clarity, ignorant. "I decided to stay."

She smiled again. Then she took a deep breath through her nose, closed her eyes, hugged the pillow tight, and uttered a single word as she drifted back to sleep.

"Good."

Beside the bed was a bonsai plant. Hedge looked at it and knew it was looking back at him. He sensed a feeling of satisfaction, of realized potential and relaxation after a long long period of tension and expectation, as though whatever it had been watching for had finally come to pass.

ABOUT THE AUTHOR

This author has held several positions in recent years, including Content Writer, Grant Writer, Obituary Clerk, and Staff Writer, and is under the false impression that these experiences have added to his character since they have not contributed much to his finances. He was awarded a BFA in Creative Writing and Journalism and a BA in Technical Communication by Bowling Green State University because they are giving and eager to make friends. He has a few scattered publications with The Circle magazine, Wild Violet, Toasted Cheese, and Lovable Losers Literary Revue, and resides in the drab, northeastern region of Ohio because it makes everything else seem fascinating, exotic, and beautiful.